Praise for Penny W~
Macavity Awar

Also by Penny Warner

Blind
Side

A Connor Westphal Mystery

Penny Warner

Perseverance Press / John Daniel & Company
Santa Barbara, California
2001

This is a work of fiction. Characters, places, and events are the product of the author's imagination or are used fictitiously. Any resemblance to real people, companies, institutions, organizations, or incidents is entirely coincidental.

10 9 8 7 6 5 4 3 2 1

A Perseverance Press Book
Published by John Daniel & Company
A division of Daniel & Daniel, Publishers, Inc.
Post Office Box 21922
Santa Barbara, California 93121
www.danielpublishing.com/perseverance

Book design: Eric Larson, Studio E Books, Santa Barbara
Cover photo: "Frogman" © 2000 Keith Brauneis

LIBRARY OF CONGRESS CATALOGING-IN-PUBLICATION DATA
Warner, Penny.
    Blind side : a Connor Westphal mystery / by Penny Warner.
        p.   cm.
    ISBN 1-880284-42-1 (alk. paper)
        1. Women journalists—Fiction.   2. Deaf women—Fiction.
    3. Frogs—Fiction.   I. Title.
    PS3573.A7659 B58 2000
    813'.54—dc21   00-008981

To Tom, Matt, and Rebecca,

a killer family

—and—

to Connie, where it all comes from

Acknowledgments

Thanks to everyone who helped with the manuscript in some form or another: Kristin Littlefield, Peggy Lucke, Lynn MacDonald, Camille Minichino, Ann Parker, Sue and Vicki Stadelhofer, and all the frogs at the Calaveras County Jumping Frog Jubilee.

A special thanks to Meredith Phillips, my wonderful editor.

"Maybe you understand frogs, and maybe you don't understand 'em; maybe you've had experience and maybe you ain't only a amature, as it were. Anyways, I've got *my* opinion, and I'll risk forty dollars that he can outjump any frog in Calaveras County."

—Mark Twain
The Celebrated Jumping Frog of Calaveras County, 1867

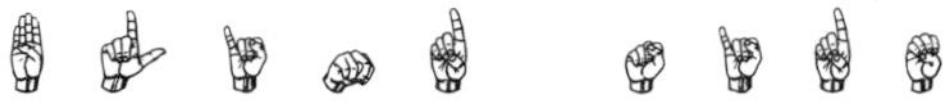

Chapter 1

AS DARKNESS RAGED torrentially outside the frog-jumping pavilion, news of Rosie the Ribbeter's untimely suicide spread through the festival like a case of viral warts....

I stopped reading the contest entry that had just arrived on my desk at the *Eureka!* newspaper office.

"Check this one out," I signed to my office assistant, Jeremiah Mercer, using finger-spelling and sign language to interpret the lines. "It's not even a poem!"

Miah grimaced. "Don't these people read the rules? So far we've gotten two short stories, three opening lines, and only seven entries that could be considered 'verse,'" he signed back. In American Sign Language, it literally came out, "People read rules—not? Have now two stories, short, three begin sentences, seven v-e-r-s-e only." Although Miah can hear, he learned ASL at the local college, and we use sign language most of the time to keep up his skills.

"And it's a stinker, isn't it?" I held my nose, the universal sign for "stink."

"Too bad." Miah signed the letters "TB."

"I agree," I signed back, moving the hand sign "Y" back and forth between us. "It's the best of the bunch. This isn't as easy as I thought it was going to be, choosing the best of the worst. Or should I say, worst of the worst?"

Miah grinned. We'd been having a great time reading entries for the newspaper's "Worst Verse" competition. I'd suggested the contest to Angels Camp Mayor Elijah Ellington to coincide with the Jumping Frog Jubilee. The unique festival is held every spring in "Frogtown," also known as the Calaveras County Fairgrounds in Angels Camp.

The amphibious event, made famous by Mark Twain's 1867 yarn, "The Celebrated Jumping Frog of Calaveras County," attracts frog fanatics from Fresno to Flat Skunk. The Mother Lode communities depend on the extra income the Jubilee harvests to support events the rest of the year.

"Have you had any more flak from Mayor Ellington?" Miah asked.

Elijah Ellington had been concerned about the "Worst Verse" contest at first, thinking I was making fun of the Jubilee. Really. How could anyone make fun of a frog-jumping contest?

"Not lately. When I told him it would bring in even more people—and therefore more money—he did a complete turnaround."

The mayor and I don't usually see eye to eye: He's a little too concerned about his public image and not enough concerned about his public for my taste. At least this time, his office and my newspaper were working together to kick off the celebrated Jubilee.

"Well, it's been totally great for the *Eureka!*," Miah signed. Although now and then he used the wrong sign or jumbled the syntax, Miah had a knack for turning spoken words into visual imagery with his long, slim fingers. And being deaf, I was grateful for his help with the newspaper tasks and the occasional interpreting chores. Miah was especially handy whenever a tight-lipped mumbler stopped by to chat.

"No kidding. Ads are up, right along with circulation. This was a brilliant idea, if I do say so myself. Guess that's why I'm chief around here," I teased.

"I thought it was my idea," Miah signed, which in American Sign Language literally read, "*My* idea, think-me!" His facial expression gave "my" and "me" just the right emphasis.

A young man of twenty-five, Miah was quick, funny, and adorable—even with the over-gelled spiky hair, silver nose ring, and the new gold tongue stud. He was smart enough to successfully run a skateboard/surfing/comic book shop, down the hall from my newspaper, but I hoped he'd do more with his talents someday. I guessed he was still trying to find himself. Much like his sixty-year-old father, Elvis Mercer, the recently divorced sheriff of Flat Skunk.

"By the way, what did you do with the ad from LEAP?" I signed, curious about how he'd handled this controversial group's official "statement." LEAP, which stood for Liberate the Exploited Amphibian Population, had been rearing its politically correct head for the past several years.

The leader of LEAP, Carrie Yates, a fifty-something environmentalist and owner of a local health care facility, had become unusually demanding this year. She'd been insisting on the resignation of Mayor Ellington if he didn't do something about the "frog exploitation." Luckily for the mayor, the frog-jumping enthusiasts vastly outnumbered the protestors. But the group still had a right to free speech—at least in my newspaper.

"I put it under the fold—two columns—with a picture of Yates kissing one of her pet frogs," Miah signed, giving the word "frogs" extra flair as he flicked two fingers under his throat. "Probably hoping it will turn into a prince. Makes good copy."

"And that's what sells newspapers." I gazed out the window at Flat Skunk's Main Street below, lined with pink-bubblegum blossoming trees and antique store signs. The downtown was filling up with tourists, frog jockeys, curious travelers, and locals. Although the Jubilee is held in Angels Camp, it's only ten miles up the road from Flat Skunk. Tourists from the San Francisco Bay Area like to drive up Highway 49 and check out all the colorful Gold Rush towns on their way to the event. And we Skunkers like to cash in on that.

Miah joined me at the window. "What are you looking at?"

"Main Street," I signed simply.

Sheriff Mercer was on his way to the Nugget Café with his young deputy, Marca Clemens. Behind them trailed our resident prospector, old Sluice Jackson, sporting a green cap with Ping-Pong ball eyes glued to the front, and two pairs of green flaps hanging down on each side to form the legs.

"Look at old Froghead," Miah signed, pointing to Sluice.

He wasn't alone. Several other townspeople and tourists sported the frog hats with T-shirts to match. Sluice had started a cottage industry, prospecting for tourists' money. Apparently this week he was making and selling frog-themed ready-to-wear.

"How's your frog doing, Miah? Eating his Wheaties and working out on the Stairmaster for the big event?"

Miah had been competing for the grand prize of five thousand dollars with his own leaping contestant ever since he was in junior high. He'd come in second a couple of times, but he'd never won the trophy. This year he was convinced he'd found the perfect champion frog.

"Yep. This time we're going to win, me and Freddy Froglegs. I'm sick of watching Dakota take home the trophy and cash every year. I'll bet he cheats. He probably feeds his mutant frog some kind of steroid cocktail." Miah finger-spelled "steroid" creatively—more like "stairod," but I managed to make it out.

According to Miah, Dakota Webster had been a friend of his all through school. But after graduation from Calaveras High, they had grown apart. In fact, it seemed they had become more distant and competitive over the years, especially when it came to the Jumping Frog Jubilee.

"How do you know you're going to win this time? Got a secret formula?" I asked.

He tried to smile mysteriously but it looked like he had a lip cramp.

"Well, good luck. I think you've got some stiff competition.

I heard some guy is bringing in a bunch of giant African speci-
mens that are supposed to be superfrogs."

"No way they'll win. They're too fat to jump far. I'm not worried. Dakota's still the only one to beat, but I've got a killer
frog, and Freddy and I have a plan. Of course, Dan has this—"

Miah suddenly looked at me as if he'd seen a ghost.
"Whoops!" he said, then clapped a hand over his mouth.

"Dan?"

Miah shrugged.

"Dan Smith? Our friend and neighbor in the office next
door? Flat Skunk's newest private investigator? The man with
the body of a construction worker and the mind of a poet?
That Dan Smith?"

Miah flushed. "I wasn't supposed to tell. Your boyfriend is
gonna kill me."

"You're kidding!" The Dan I knew and loved was too sen-
sible to compete with a bunch of kids—or men who still acted
like kids. Especially in a friggin' frog-jumping contest. "He's
entering a frog?"

I think Miah mistook my surprise for interest. He signed
with new energy. "Yep. Named it Ribicop. You know, like
Robocop? Get it?"

I got it. But not the reason why Dan would participate in
the silly games. And hide it from me. Men.

"Wait'll I see him…" I headed back to the computer to get
some work done, but Miah waved something white within my
peripheral vision.

"Hey, here's one." Miah held up a sheet of paper. I watched
his lips carefully as he read the note without signing.

A frog named François jumped so far
When taking off from Paris,
He hit an airplane, tumbled down,
And croaked in Calaveras….

I snorted. "Great one. Like I said, picking a winner won't

be easy. But we're down to the wire, Miah. The opening ceremony for the Jubilee is tonight, and we have to present the Worst Verse award right after Mayor Ellington makes his welcoming remarks. Of course, that could last up to two hours."

Miah wasn't watching my signs. His attention was on another envelope that had apparently gone unnoticed under the pile of papers that had collected on his desk.

"Uh-oh. One more." Miah tore open the envelope.

"Okay, but this is the last one. Then we choose."

"Here goes." I watched Miah's lips.

Mr. Toad took a wild ride
Across the finish line,
But waiting there was a frying pan,
That sautéed him with white wine ....

"I love it! What do you say? Do we have a winner?" I signed.

Miah nodded with his head and his fist. "You're right. It's a killer." He signed "killer" by twisting an imaginary knife under his left hand.

"Who wrote it? I have to notify the winner to show up tonight and receive the award—not to mention, get a shirt size for a custom-made frog hat and matching T-shirt, compliments of Sluice Jackson."

"Wow," Miah signed, shaking his hand in the air.

"Someone we know?"

"Not exactly."

"Who, then?"

"The name is Del Ores Montez. Maybe a relative of Del Rey's?"

I took the entry from Miah and reread it. Del Rey Montez, our local mortician and my good friend, had mentioned a sister once. But I thought she was in some kind of institution. For what reason, I couldn't remember.

"Montez is a common name around here. Could be someone else." I checked the return address on the envelope:

Memory Kingdom Memorial Park. "Then again, maybe you're right. Guess I'll go find out."

I picked up my backpack and headed over.

"Del Rey?" I called out. I pulled the heavy front door shut behind me and entered the Disneyesque funeral home. The previous owner had operated a chain of mortuaries, each with a different thematic design. The one in Flat Skunk featured billowing clouds painted on the walls, lush velvet antique settees and love seats in the foyer, and giant paper flowers stuck inside heart-shaped boxes. Snow White would have been very comfortable here.

"Hi, Del Rey," I said to my friend, as she appeared from behind a velvet curtain at the back of the entryway. "New outfit?"

"I'm sorry. I'm not Del Rey. My name is Del Ores."

I stood with my mouth open like a frog waiting for a fly. The woman looked nearly identical to Del Rey—plump pink cheeks, dark curly hair, and Betty Boop lips. As I stared at her, I realized only the eyes were different. Del Rey's sparkled; this woman's eyes were dark and smoky.

"I...uh..." I was taken aback for a few seconds.

Del Ores seemed to sense my hesitation. "Del Rey's not here right now. May I help you?" She didn't make eye contact but seemed to be staring at something behind me. I turned around to see what it was but noticed nothing particularly eye-catching.

"You're Del Rey's sister?" I asked, certain she was. Her face brightened.

"Yes! I guess what they say is true. We look a lot alike, but our personalities are so different, it's sometimes hard to believe we're related." She spoke with a smile, but still didn't meet my eyes. I wondered if she was just terribly shy. If this was the sister who'd been living in an institution, maybe she hadn't had much social contact.

"I'm a good friend of your sister's. My name is Connor West-phal. I'm glad to meet you—" I reached out for a hand-shake.

Del Ores stood only four feet away from me, but she made no effort to meet my hand.

And then I remembered what Del Rey had told me about her sister. Del Ores was blind!

Momentarily flustered, I pulled myself together and stepped forward to close the gap. I grasped the blind woman's hand and shook it.

Just then Del Rey burst through the door. Del Ores started at the noise.

"Connor! Hi! I see you've met my sister."

"Yes —" I started to say, but Del Rey cut me off.

"Have you heard the news?" she continued, looking concerned. Her rosy cheeks were even more flushed than usual.

"Of course I have. I'm the one responsible. How did you find out?" I was stunned that Del Rey already knew about Del Ores winning the contest. I'd kill Miah when I got back to the office. That would make two men I had to kill today.

"*You're* responsible? But—"

"It's my contest. I get to choose the winner. And—"

"I'm not talking about the contest! I'm talking about Dakota Webster!"

I paused. "What about him?" It was taking me a few seconds to catch up with Del Rey. We'd been on different pages.

"He's dead!"

"Dakota?" I said in disbelief.

"No! Buford!"

"Del Rey! You're not making any sense! Who's Buford? And what's Dakota got to do with this?"

"Buford the Bullfrog is Dakota's champion frog. Dakota found him a little while ago in his pond—croaked!"

Chapter 2

"CROAKED? NICE CHOICE of words, Del Rey," I said, dropping into a nearby faux Louis-the-Whatever chair. Buford the Bullfrog was dead. Del Rey's sister was blind. And I was experiencing information overload.

"How did it croak—er, die?" I faced Del Rey to read her lips, but she was already engaged in conversation with her sister. With my back to them both, I hadn't noticed.

I watched Del Ores as she chatted with Del Rey, never meeting her sister's eyes, and felt a sudden sense of sadness that surprised and bothered me. I didn't understand when hearing people felt sorry for me—and I hated it. But not being able to see... I couldn't imagine such a consuming handicap. One of my biggest fears, being deaf, is the possibility of losing my vision. I would not make a good Helen Keller.

I caught a hand waving in my peripheral vision. Del Rey was trying to get my attention.

"Sheriff Locke is threatening to postpone, even cancel, the opening ceremonies for the Jumping Frog Jubilee!"

"You're kidding! Just because a frog died? That doesn't make sense."

"It does when there might be murder involved," she said.

"Murder?" I asked. "I thought you said a frog died. That's sabotage, maybe, but not murder."

"It might be, if the frog's jockey calls it murder."

"You mean to tell me Dakota Webster thinks his champion

frog was deliberately killed? Why? To keep him from winning again? Jeez. This friendly little competition is suddenly taking on a few warts. What did Sheriff Mercer say?"

"I don't know. I just heard about all this from Jilda, down at the Nugget Café. You better talk to Sheriff Mercer himself if you want the dirt for your newspaper."

I hoisted my backpack. "I will. It would be disastrous if the event was cancelled. I wonder if Dakota has any proof. You know, like gunshot wounds or rope burns around the neck?"

Del Rey grinned. Del Ores looked a bit bewildered. I suddenly remembered why I was there in the first place.

"Oh! I almost forgot! The reason I came here was to tell you—and Del Ores—the good news. She won —" I said to Del Rey, then forced myself to address Del Ores. I realized I had not been speaking directly to her. The same thing often happened to me. "You won the Worst Verse contest!"

"I did?" Del Ores's face lit up. Her eyes flitted back and forth like a metronome set for triple time. She looked positively delighted. "Oh dearie, I've never won anything in my life!"

Dearie?

"Way to go, Dodo! I told you you could do it!" Del Rey said.

"Dodo?" I repeated aloud. "That's not a very nice name for your sister. Especially since she's just beat out over twenty-five people for the award."

The sisters laughed. Del Ores spoke first. "Oh, that's just my nickname. She calls me Dodo, 'cause the initials of my name are 'D O.'"

"And she calls me Deeree, 'cause mine are D R," said Del Rey.

So, what I had seen as "dearie" had actually been "Deeree." I nodded in semi-comprehension, then realized Del Ores couldn't see the acknowledgment. I said aloud, "That's really...cute. Anyway, I guess I have a new glitch to work out—whether this contest is a 'go' tonight. I'll talk to Sheriff

Mercer and see what's up. But I can't imagine they'd actually cancel the whole Jubilee. Bazillions of people are already here and raring to go. Besides, it's just a dead frog."

"Wait until Carrie Yates and her frog fanatics find out. What are they calling themselves? Toaders? Lepers? Mouth Breathers?" Del Rey asked.

"LEAPers. 'Liberate the Exploited Amphibian Population.' You're right. Carrie's going to have an I-told-you-so fit about this. But right now, that's not my problem."

I faced Del Ores and instinctively reached out my hand as I turned to leave. "Congratulations again, Del Ores."

She ignored my gesture. I quickly touched her on the shoulder instead, but she winced, not expecting the intrusion. I headed out the mortuary door feeling like an idiot.

I pondered the "murder" of Buford the Bullfrog on my way over to Sheriff Mercer's office. Tourists crowded the sidewalks, killing time in our quaint boutiques and keeping cool in our old-fashioned ice cream parlors until the festivities began.

Flat Skunk has plenty to offer the out-of-towners on their way to the Jubilee: gold mining expeditions, quaint coffee shops, and antique stores overflowing with overpriced Coke bottles, out-of-print magazines, and how-to-strike-it-rich guidebooks. They don't still call the Mother Lode towns along Highway 49 the "gold chain" for no reason.

I passed a young boy training his frog in the town gazebo. Training amounted to holding the frog by the scruff of its neck and dropping it on a small pad, then leaping up and down on all fours and screaming at the critter to make it jump. In the Jubilee, the frog would have three jumps to make the most distance. The world-record jump was set in May of 1986 by Rosie the Ribbiter. It leapt an impressive 21 feet, 5.75 inches.

But aside from scaring the critters to death with all that

screaming, how would someone kill a frog? Step on it? Can't exactly drown it. I'd have to do some amphibian research for my story before the *Eureka!* went to press.

As I approached the sheriff's building, someone grabbed my shoulders from behind. I jumped like a terrified toad. I reminded myself of Del Ores wincing at my touch.

"Jesus!" I turned to face my attacker. It was Dan Smith, interrupting my murder scenarios. He stood there in his jeans and T-shirt, his cowboy boots and baseball cap, stroking his trimmed salt-and-pepper beard. "Would you stop doing that? You know how I hate it!"

"What? I called your name but you didn't answer." He grinned. He appeared to be on his way to his office from the general vicinity of the Nugget Café.

"Very funny. Some day I'm going to show you what it's like to be crept up on and grabbed."

"I might like it, depending on where you grab." The grin spread wider across his face.

"I understand you're entering a frog in the jubilee?" That wiped the smile off his face. Busted.

Dan shrugged. "I was just fooling around. I thought it might be kind of fun, you know..." He changed the subject, distracting me by using sign language. "So what's the rush?" Granted, the words looked a little contorted in his thick, muscular fingers, but I got the gist of it. He tended to use SEE signs—Seeing Exact English—which is a more literal translation of English into sign language. Most hearing people prefer it.

"Good signing. You've been practicing." I was afraid to correct his one mistake—he'd used the word "salad" instead of "rush." I figured if I criticized him too much, he'd quit signing altogether. Better to let him get a few words wrong than to have him give up because of some minor but hilarious errors.

He flexed his muscular arm, kissed his fingertips, and brought them forward, the sign for "thanks." Then he shook his hands out. "That's enough signing for today. I'm starting to get carpal tunnel syndrome."

I laughed. "You need to relax your hands when you sign. Try not to be so tense. Let them glide from one letter or sign to the next, like this."

I finger-spelled his name—D-A-N-I-E-L-S-M-I-T-H—in one long flow of finger movement.

He shook his head. "I saw the 'D' and the 'H' and that's it. You're too fast."

"That reminds me. I'm in a hurry."

"Where are you off to?"

"Sheriff Mercer's office. I heard there's been a...death that may affect the opening ceremony of the Frog Jubilee tonight. You hear any dirt at the Nugget?"

"Maybe," he said slyly. "After all, I am a private investigator now. A gumshoe. An ex-flatfoot walking the mean streets of Flat Skunk. But I'm not taking the rap for you, baby—"

I rolled my eyes. "Enough! You know how sexy you are when you do Bogey, especially when you hold your lip in like that and I can't lip-read you, but I haven't got time for that now. Tell me if you know anything about this dead frog rumor."

"All I know is, Butch the Frog, or whatever his name was, was allegedly murdered—in cold blood—according to his jockey, Dakota Webster."

"I already know that. Got anything else alleged? Like how he was allegedly murdered? And who the alleged killer is?" I said, mocking his police jargon. Even after he left the New York City Police Department, the cop in him stayed.

"Only that this Dakota guy thinks his frog was poisoned. But I can't say much more. Client-gumshoe privilege, you know."

"You don't mean—" I looked at him, stunned.

He nodded. "I'm on the case."

"You're kidding me!"

"Nope. Got a call on my cell phone at the Nugget just a few

minutes ago. Mr. Webster asked me to meet him at the sheriff's office."

If it hadn't been so ludicrous, I'd have laughed.

No one was laughing at the sheriff's office. Sheriff Mercer sat at his desk, tapping his pencil. Dakota Webster stood opposite him, pointing. But he wasn't pointing at the sheriff. His finger was directed at Miah, the sheriff's son, who slumped in a large wooden chair across the room.

"C.W.!" The sheriff stood up. He actually looked relieved to see me. That didn't happen often. Guess he preferred my company to his current guests. "Hey, Dan," he added.

Dan shook hands with Sheriff Mercer and nodded to Miah, and we both turned our attention to Dakota. That young man, about Miah's age, wore his hair short and neat, unlike Miah's spiky style. He was taller than my five-eight by several inches and looked like he worked out at the gym. Physically, the guys seemed as if they could have been brothers. But Dakota's outfit took me by surprise. Instead of baggy jeans and a logo T-shirt like Miah wore, Dakota had on hospital greens.

"You must be Dakota Webster?" Dan reached out and shook the young man's hand.

"Yeah." He turned to Sheriff Mercer and said, "Sheriff, this is my private dick."

I know I blushed. I saw the guys all stifle grins—except Dakota.

"He's going to investigate what happened to Buford. And I know he'll dig up the truth 'cause he's got no one to protect!" Dakota turned his attention from the sheriff to glare at Miah. "Come on, Mr. Smith. We have some details to talk over."

With that, Dakota Webster stormed out of the office. Dan gave a shrug, waved us good-bye, and followed the angry man out the door.

I looked at the sheriff, then Miah, puzzled. "What's he talking about? What's going on?"

Miah just shook his head. The sheriff frowned and dropped back into his chair. After a few chin rubs with the back of his hand, he spoke.

"I guess you've heard the basics. Webster's champion frog died...suspiciously..." he glanced at Miah, but Miah was staring at his athletic shoes "...some time today while Webster was out. He says someone entered his backyard, found Buford in the lily pond he'd built especially for his frogs, and poisoned the water. Buford was the only frog in the pond at the time."

"Has he got proof? I mean, how does he know the pond water was poisoned? Maybe Buford had a heart attack from all the pressure of the contest or something." I was trying to lighten things up a bit, but I wasn't getting much of a response from the Mercer men.

"I sent Deputy Clemens to check it out. But now Dakota's gone and got himself a P.I. I didn't realize it was going to be Dan."

"Well, Dan will get to the bottom of it, and fairly, you know that. In the meantime, is the Jubilee still on for tonight?"

The sheriff glanced at Miah again, but Miah still didn't meet his eyes. He was busy staring at his feet. Maybe he was worried about the contest being cancelled, too. I knew he'd worked hard training his own frog for the jump.

"So far it's still on, but I'm not sure that's such a good idea. No reason why we can't postpone the opening ceremonies until tomorrow morning, but the committee insisted. Mayor Ellington convinced them there was no good reason to shut it down. And Peyton agrees." Peyton Locke was the sheriff of Angels Camp—and Sheriff Mercer's first girlfriend since his wife had left him two years ago.

"Good. I mean, I'm sorry for Dakota, and if someone is tampering with the frog contestants, we need to find out about it. But we can't really close down the entire event at this point."

"Well, it's on for now anyway. We'll see if my deputy turns

up anything in that pond. And we'll see what Dan finds out. I'll tell you, he's got his hands full taking on this case for a guy like Dakota Webster."

"Why, what's the guy like? And why was he wearing those pajamas?" I really didn't know much more about him, except that he and Miah were no longer friends.

Miah started talking for the first time since I'd arrived, signing as he spoke. "He's training to be a nurse over at the Mother Lode Hospital."

"I take it you don't like him much anymore," I said.

"I don't dislike him," he said. "I hate him." He signed "hate" by flicking his two middle fingers.

"That's a little harsh. I thought the two of you were good friends in high school."

"That's history. Before I knew what a jerk he was."

"So what kind of jerk is he?" I asked.

Miah glanced at his father and looked away. The sheriff rubbed his chin until I thought he might never grow a beard again, then he said, "He's the kind that accuses my son of killing his damn frog."

Chapter 3

I'D NEVER SEEN MIAH so upset. He's usually an even-tempered, laid-back kind of guy, often the calm one when crises arise at the newspaper. His father is the more emotional one in the family. I had a feeling there was something more behind this accusation of Dakota's.

"Miah, why does Dakota think you killed his frog?"

"Because he hates me as much as I hate him. He probably killed his own frog, just to have something to blame on me!"

"Miah, you don't honestly think—"

"I wouldn't put it past him! He's done a lot of things that would surprise people around here." Miah stood up, hunched his jacket over his shoulders, and fled the office, leaving the sheriff and me to stare at the slammed-shut door.

I turned to Sheriff Mercer. "What's that all about?"

The sheriff rubbed his chin. It was starting to turn red from abuse. "It's a long story, C.W. Started when they were seniors in high school. They'd been friends for years. Grew up together. Got along great. But something happened that year...." The sheriff drifted off.

I waited for him to continue. When he seemed hopelessly lost in his thoughts, I brought him back. "Sheriff?"

"Huh? Oh. Where was I?"

"In high school," I reminded him.

"Yeah. So anyways, there was this girl."

I nodded. *"Cherchez la femme."*

"Huh?" The sheriff seemed to be scratching behind his ear. I had a hunch he was fiddling with his new hearing aid. I didn't think it would help him understand French.

"I said, it's always a woman, isn't it, Sheriff?"

"Seems like it. Anyway, Miah was dating this girl named Simonie. Simonie Scott. Cute little thing. Cheerleader. School social director or something like that. Organized all the dances and stuff. Worked as a candy-striper at the hospital after school."

I didn't recognize the name, but the type was familiar. Bet she was a blonde. Don't go there, Connor, I told myself. Those grueling high school years are way over.

"Dakota was always a little jealous of Miah. Miah played sports, did well in school, was popular. Dakota kind of hung onto his coattails, especially in high school. Then for some reason, right before graduation, Simonie changed. She broke up with Miah and started going out with Dakota."

"Uh-oh," I said, familiar with the lifelong complications of the boy-meets-girl, girl-meets-another-boy, girl-breaks-up-with-first-boy-and-goes-with-new-boy scenario. It had happened to me just before I moved to Flat Skunk, only in reverse. In fact, it was one of the reasons I'd left San Francisco and moved north. Men. "And Miah was upset."

"If he was, he didn't show it openly. But the friendship cooled between the two guys. Then they took their competition to another level."

"The Jumping Frog Contest."

"Yep. You'd have thought they were competing for Olympic gold, although the prize money isn't bad. Every year for the past five years these two have gone head-to-head for the championship. And every year, Dakota takes home the trophy and prize money."

"So in Miah's mind, Dakota ended up with his girlfriend *and* his trophy. Think it's enough reason to kill a championship frog?"

The sheriff looked down at his desk. I realized then he didn't know for sure if his son had done the deed or not. Well, I did.

"Sheriff! Miah's your son. He'd never do anything under-handed like that."

"I know, I know. It's just that..." He paused, rubbed his chin again. He'd have to get some Mercurochrome on that soon.

"What?"

"He doesn't have an alibi. He was by himself all afternoon. Said he was working with his frog. But he's certainly got the best motive."

"What about a weapon? Does your deputy know for sure if there was poison in the pond?"

"Not yet. We're getting the water tested. But my guess is, it's probably something anyone could have bought over the counter. Like rat poison."

"Well, Miah didn't do it. We just have to prove who did."

"We?" The sheriff eyed me. "You got a frog in your pocket?"

"Huh?"

"I said...never mind. It's just an expression, sort of. Any-way, there is no 'we' here, C.W. I'll handle it. I'm just venting."

I hate it when hearing people won't explain a phrase or a joke. Deaf people miss a lot of the subtleties of the English language. I was left out much of the time in high school when girls told jokes I didn't get or used slang that made no sense to me.

"Well, I have to write up something for the *Eureka!*, and I'd like to get it right. Especially before the *Mother Lode Monitor* gets the story, not to mention the wire services. Something like this could make the national news. Luckily, I have a slight advantage since my paper comes out on Saturdays. The weekday *Monitor* won't have anything until Monday."

"Yeah, but if you do a rush job, they'll still beat you to a better story."

"That's why we're going to find out what really happened, Sheriff. Start combing your hair. I'm going to put you on the front page, top of the fold."

Sheriff Mercer reflexively smoothed down his sparse hair. The man was a sucker for publicity. It was his Achilles' heel. Mine was getting the story.

"Is Dakota still seeing this Simone person?"

"Her name's Simonie. *Sim*-mon-ee."

"*Sim*-mon-ee," I repeated, enunciating carefully. Lip-reading him, I hadn't seen the extra syllable and assumed it was the standard French name.

"And yes, as far as I know, Dakota is still seeing her. I saw them together at the fairgrounds earlier."

"Do you know where I can find her? I'd like to talk to her."

"I think she's a nurse, too, over at the Mother Lode Hos—"

The door burst open. Three women and two men attempted to fit their bodies and their large hand-drawn signs simultaneously through the single-person doorway. One woman got bonked on the head by a sign in front of her, while another sign was bent in half, not quite making it through the small opening. I could just make out the printed information waving in front of my face:

FREE OUR FROGS!

LIBERATE THE EXPLOITED AMPHIBIAN POPULATION

DEAD FROGS CAN'T JUMP

CROAKED IN CALAVERAS

Only in Flat Skunk, I thought.

Sheriff Mercer stood up, waving his hands to calm down the agitated mini-mob. "Hold on! Hold on! What's this all about?"

"Sheriff! Enough is enough. We warned you something like this might happen! And now it has!"

Carrie Yates, owner of the GetWell health care facility, did most of the talking, although it looked like she was screaming. Her red hair looked inflamed, and it set off her mouth, opened so wide it looked contorted. But she kept the words simple so I could make out most of what she had to say, unfortunately. Middle-aged and recently remarried to a newcomer in town, Burnett Pike, Carrie seemed to be the leader of the pack. Her unlikely husband, tan, thin, neatly dressed but stooped, stood nearby, grimacing and silent.

"What are you talking about, Carrie?" Sheriff Mercer said. "We've gone over this a million times. The frogs aren't being mistreated—"

Carrie's drooping eyes lit up. Her face, worn with age or perhaps years of anger, glowed red with her current passion, nearly matching her hair. The dye job was an obvious attempt to look as young as her new husband, who seemed at least ten years her junior. "Oh, is that right, Sheriff Mercer? Well, what about *murder*?"

Uh-oh, I thought. Word spreads in Flat Skunk faster than a case of viral warts. Now where had I heard that?

"Calm down, Carrie. Everything's under control. We don't know that Dakota's frog was murdered. It's just a rumor at this point."

"And if it was murder?" Her mouth pulled back into a vicious slit.

"Then we'll find out what happened and deal with it. But this kind of thing doesn't help. In fact, you're taking up valuable time I could be spending on the investigation. Now take your signs—"

The woman wouldn't take "get out" for an answer. She was too enraged to hear anything the sheriff had to say. I watched her body language, especially her hands as they gripped her sign until her knuckles turned a pearly white.

"Your son is a murderer—" In the middle of her latest verbal onslaught, she turned her sign upside down and raised the stick.

"Carrie!" I caught the word as her husband jumped out from the crowd. Burnett held down her arms, effectively lowering the potential weapon. She fought to raise her hands again, but he overpowered her, half hugging her, half wrestling the sign from her. He wrenched it from her grasp, then threw it to the floor.

"Sheriff, watch out!" I screamed, as Carrie reared up and

lunged for Sheriff Mercer. But Burnett tackled her from behind and brought her down to the floor. The crowd of LEAPers appeared stunned at the outburst. They backed up quietly, waiting to see what the crazed woman would do next.

She did nothing. She lay there on the floor, face down, her husband on top of her.

"Is she all right?" I asked, kneeling down.

Surprised at the attack, the sheriff had pulled out his billy club. He gestured the crowd out the door, then turned to the human pile on the floor.

Burnett Pike looked up pleadingly. "Please, she's...she's under a lot of stress, Sheriff. I'm sorry. She hasn't taken her medication...." He sat up, stroking his wife's hair as she lay trembling. She was crying.

Burnett reached into his pocket and brought out a handful of pills. I got a cup of water from the bathroom, while Burnett helped his wife to sit up. She took the pills and drank them down with the water I brought her.

After a few moments, Burnett helped the now complaisant woman to her feet, cuddling her against his shoulder.

"Sheriff, I hope you won't press charges. I promise it won't happen again."

I think the sheriff was too dumbfounded to speak. He just shook his head and motioned with his billy club for them to leave.

Burnett glanced at me. "She's taken this frog death awfully hard. Try to understand." He guided her to the door, then turned back to Sheriff Mercer.

"I'm sorry. I'm sure it's her medication. She hasn't been well these past few months. But I'll get it sorted out." He backed out the door and closed it behind him.

The sheriff shook his head. "Frog fanatics. That's all I need."

Only in Flat Skunk.

I was about to head out the door myself when I caught sight of Mayor Ellington through the window, pushing his way through the dispersing crowd and heading toward the office. Can't leave now, I thought. Things are heating up. And that makes good copy.

"Sheriff?" I said, stepping back in.

"What now, C.W.?"

"You're about to get another visitor."

"Now who?"

"Mayor Ellington."

"Oh, shit!" The sheriff threw down the pencil he'd just picked up. "What the hell does he want?"

I stood aside as the mayor pushed past me. "Hi, Mayor Ellington," I said cordially.

He nodded at me, then at Sheriff Mercer. "Sheriff."

"Mayor Ellington. To what do I owe this unexpected visit?"

I sometimes wondered how the mayor got elected in Angels Camp. Short, overweight, balding, and loud, Ellington was not well liked, except by his fraternal brethren. He once held the questionable position of Noble Grand Humbug of E. Clampus Vitus, a long-standing secret men's lodge that promoted "the betterment of widders and orphans—especially widders." But the Clampers, now mostly dedicated to hanging plaques and drinking beer, was a strong constituency in these parts.

Besides that, the mayor hated to lose anything — especially elections and the income generated by the Frog Jubilee. I knew why he was here. To make sure the show would go on. If it didn't, Angels Camp, Flat Skunk, and the neighboring towns would take a substantial loss to their economy. The mayor in particular needed the support, both financially and politically. It was a fact I often noted in the *Eureka!*

And the mayor didn't care much for that.

"I need to speak with you, Sheriff, about this recent development."

The mayor turned to face me. "Alone, if you don't mind."

I waited for the sheriff's cue; he nodded. "If you'll excuse us, C.W., it looks like Mayor Ellington and I have some business to discuss."

I glared at the sheriff. He knew I wanted to see what the mayor had to say. Now I'd have to pump him later. And pump him I would.

"Sure, Sheriff," I said stiffly. "I've got a newspaper to get out, and the headlines are coming fast and furious. If you'll excuse me, Mayor, Sheriff?" I started to back out when the mayor grabbed my arm.

"You better not be printing anything about that frog death, Westphal, or you may find yourself without a newspaper someday!"

I stared at the mayor, stunned at his overt threat. "Ever heard of freedom of the press?" I asked. I slammed the door shut on his fat face.

And then I sneaked over to the sheriff's back window to read the mayor's lips as he ranted and raved. Sometimes being deaf—and knowing how to lip-read—has its advantages.

Chapter 4

I WISHED THE sheriff would clean his windows more often. It looked like they hadn't been touched since winter ended. I had to struggle to read the mayor's thin lips through the smeared, gritty panes. And I hate thin lips. It's like trying to lip-read a frog.

"...contest...can't...poor taste..." was about all I made out between the thin pink lines Mayor Ellington called a mouth. Bird-doo, old rain streaks, and cobwebs on the windowpane didn't help.

I could see Sheriff Mercer shaking his head and arguing, but the words were mostly incomprehensible. He stood sideways to me, which is a challenge even when the lips are not obstructed. I concentrated on the mayor and tried to fill in the gaps.

"...can't cancel...money loss...newspaper..."

I was fairly certain Mayor Ellington was talking about my newspaper and my contest. He probably wanted the Worst Verse competition dropped from the opening ceremonies. He didn't like it when I made fun of local events in print.

Something touched my back. I spun around.

"Dan! Shit! This is the second time today you've sneaked up on me!" I took a breath. "I thought you were in council with your client. What are you doing here?"

"Trying to keep you from being arrested."

"What? I haven't done anything. Is there a law against reading lips through a windowpane?"

"There's a law against spying, being a Peeping Tom, acting under suspicious circumstances, loitering...."

"All right, all right! I was just...checking on the sheriff to make sure he was okay. The mayor looked pretty pissed off when he got here."

"I think the sheriff can take care of himself."

I stepped away from the window and followed Dan toward the street.

"So what's going on?" he said when we reached the sidewalk.

"I'll show you mine if you show me yours. What did Dakota say?"

"Now, Connor. You know I can't say anything. Client-gumshoe privilege."

"Would you quit calling yourself a gumshoe! You sound like a bad detective movie. At least, tell me if he has anything he can prove against Miah."

Dan shook his head. I took it to mean Dakota had little to say, instead of the possibility that Dan wasn't going to answer me.

"How about the mayor? What's up with him?" Dan asked.

"From what I gathered through a filthy window and flat-liner lips, he wants to throw out the Worst Verse contest. Thinks it's in poor taste, now that a frog has met his death under suspicious circumstances. You know the mayor. He doesn't have a sense of humor when it comes to community events."

"Are you going to drop it?"

"Are you nuts? I've been working on this contest for weeks! We finally have a winner, a very deserving person who happens to be blind, and we're going to announce that tonight at the opening ceremonies. My paper has done a lot to support this event. They owe me."

"You're not worried about the Froggers?"

"Who? Oh, you mean the LEAPers? No. They're sort of out of commission at the moment. Leadership problems."

"So you're going ahead with the contest?"

"Damn right."

Dan and I took a dinner break at the Nugget Café before the 7:00 P.M. opening ceremonies. We had to wait several minutes in the crowded doorway before getting one of the ten booths; the place was packed with out-of-towners. Even the counter stools were full. I didn't recognize anyone except Jilda, who worked part-time when she wasn't at the hair salon doing nails, and Mama Cody, the owner, cook, head waitress, janitor, and manager of the Nugget. Good for business, but bad for us townies who were used to half-empty diners, plenty of parking, and familiar faces.

We didn't have much time. The fairgrounds would open at 6:00 P.M. with food vendors, souvenir sellers, and a kiddies' jumping frog contest to lure in the families—and the money. After the mayor's welcoming remarks, I was scheduled to read a few of the best of the worst and award a T-shirt and prize money to the winner.

"Where's Miah now?" Dan said, between bites of Mama Cody's meatloaf. He licked a bit from his mustache and it gave me a sensual chill.

I shrugged, my mouth full of BLT. When it was clear of food, I said, "He stormed off soon after Dakota left. Seemed really upset. The sheriff is worried about him—Miah has no alibi and he has a motive. But I shouldn't be telling you this. You're the opposition."

Dan took a long swallow of his beer. "I haven't actually taken the case."

I must have looked surprised. Dan grinned.

"First of all, I'm not sure there is a case. The sheriff is checking the pond water for poison. I told Dakota I'd look around for anything that might be pertinent, no charge. The main thing is to find out what really happened. Then we'll go from there."

"So he's not officially your client?"

He started to shake his head, then stopped. "Hold on a minute. That doesn't mean I'm going to tell you anything," he said. "I'm just saying, I haven't decided yet. And in the meantime, I'm going to look into it."

I nodded. "Cool...so, did you find out anything yet?"

Dan laughed. "Since I've been on the case for about an hour, I've learned that the meatloaf is a little overcooked, the beer is warm, and there are too many people in Flat Skunk this weekend."

"I meant *information!*"

The couple next to us got up and left the booth. The red leatherette cushions had barely filled with air before two more people sat down. I didn't recognize the two women, but both were attractive. The younger one, twenty-something, too thin, too much blond hair, wore a nurse's uniform much like Dakota's, only with little bunny rabbits all over it. The other woman, forty or so, was dressed in a severe business suit and sported several gold bracelets and rings. Mother and daughter? I wondered, although there was no real physical resemblance. Except for the scowls. They both had the same expression on their otherwise pretty faces.

Dan, noticing my gaze, turned and watched them sit down. When he turned back, I also had a scowl.

"You'll get a neck ache doing that," I said.

He grinned. "Sorry. Reflex."

Men. "Do you know them?"

He nodded. "The nurse. Met her today, as a matter of fact."

I suddenly felt a rush of jealousy. And why not? The woman was a knockout, and Dan was a very good-looking, red-blooded male.

"Did she treat you for a hangnail or something?" I knew my sarcasm was showing and I hated myself for it. But I couldn't help it.

"You're jealous!"

"I am not! What's to be jealous about? She's half your age, probably never heard of Holden Caulfield or *M*A*S*H*, and besides, she's a lesbian."

"Oh, really? How can you tell?"

"We know these things," I said, trying to sound mysterious.

"That will come as a big surprise to Dakota."

I blinked. "What do you mean?"

"He's dating her."

I flushed. "Oh. Well, I meant politically...."

"I like it when you're jealous. Your eyes turn green and your face lights up like a tomato and—"

"Shut up. Now tell me about her."

"Her name's Simonie Scott. She's twenty-four. Works as a geriatric nurse at the Mother Lode Hospital. She hangs out with Dakota."

Miah's old girlfriend was apparently still Dakota's current girlfriend. I took a long look at her, until she caught me staring, then I returned my focus to Dan. I filled him in with the details of Miah's and Dakota's past rivalry over Simonie.

"Not surprised. She's a looker," said Dan. "But something tells me the relationship is on the outs. The two of them argued during most of our conversation. She kept interrupting, saying Miah killed Dakota's frog, over and over. She really seems to have it in for Miah. I got the feeling Dakota was heavily influenced by her."

"I have a feeling there's more to this than Miah has let on. Who's the older woman?" I nodded toward the booth.

"Don't know. She's wearing a hospital nameplate, too, but I can't make out the name."

"I'd really like to talk with Simonie about Miah. I wonder—"

Just then another woman appeared at the table. Also a nurse, but a few years older than Simonie, maybe in her late twenties or early thirties. She, too, was attractive, but big-boned, slightly overweight, with curly black hair and a few blemishes. She held a glass of Mama Cody's famous red punch in one hand.

The two women sitting at the booth visibly stiffened when they saw the newcomer. The standing woman said something I couldn't make out, which garnered a response from Simonie. All I caught was "...Dakota isn't interested..." before I lost the rest, thanks to the constant bobbing of her head. But whatever Simonie was saying, it was passionate.

The curly-haired nurse said something back. Then Simonie looked stunned, as if she'd been slapped. She jumped up, her mouth and eyes wide open, and looked down.

Blocked by the table, I tried to stand in an attempt to see what happened. The front of Simonie's cute bunny uniform was covered in red.

Blood?

"Oops. Sorry," I saw the newcomer say. She didn't look sorry. She held an empty glass upside down in front of her. Drops of red liquid dripped onto the table. It was clear the woman had deliberately dumped her glass of punch on Simonie.

I thought it might become an all-out food fight, but the curly-haired woman spun around and marched out of the diner.

Jilda rushed over with a handful of paper towels gripped in her inch-long iridescent blue fingernails. "Oh, that punch will never come out," she said, as she tried to mop up the mess.

"Just stop!" Simonie said, her face contorted with anger. She headed for the bathroom, leaving her companion alone and bewildered at the booth.

"Did you catch anything?" I signed to Dan, not wanting to be overheard.

"Something about not getting Dakota, but that's it," he signed back.

I nodded. "That man brings out the worst in people, doesn't he?"

Dan and I arrived at Frogtown at 6:30, joining the masses of humanity as they streamed through the ticket booth entrance. I had a press pass, but Dan had to pay, so I told him I'd catch up with him at the stage where the opening ceremonies would be held.

Zigzagging through the throng of frog-lovers, I made my way to the center of the fairgrounds. Down at the stage area, Mayor Ellington was giving orders to assistants dressed as Old West cowboys. It didn't seem like a good time to confront him about the contest, but I had no choice. We were due to begin in half an hour. I headed onto the stage.

"Mayor Ellington," I said, after it looked like he'd finished yelling at an electrician.

He spun around. "What is it—oh, you. What do you want?"

I ignored his abrupt attitude. "What time exactly will I be announcing the winner of the Worst Verse contest, Mayor?" In other words, how long would his boring speech take?

"I'm sorry, Ms. Westphal. Hasn't anyone told you? We're canceling that part of the event."

"What? But Mayor, you can't cancel it. You have no right. You'd be disappointing all those people who—"

"Can't be helped, Westphal. After the death of Dakota Webster's frog, I think it would be tasteless and insensitive to make fun of our webbed friends. I'm sure you understand—"

"I do not understand! My contest has nothing to do with that frog's death, which I'm sure will turn out to be an accident. My newspaper has done a lot for this Jubilee and—"

We kept cutting each other off. It was his turn. "My decision is final, Westphal. The contest is off. Now if you'll excuse me—"

He walked away, leaving me standing there in the middle of the stage with no encore.

He had no right. Decisions were made by committee, not by one person. The sheriff was going to hear about this.

Speak of the devil, Sheriff Mercer suddenly appeared from out of the crowd, accompanied by his new paramour, Sheriff

Peyton Locke from Angels Camp. The two sheriffs had been dating for several months. Although they'd tried their best not to let anyone know, everyone did, of course. The same ages, with the same interests, they made a darling twosome. At the moment, however, they didn't look like a happy couple. I wondered if there was trouble in Dodge.

"Sheriff—" I called out to him from the stage and waved my hands to catch his attention. He might not be able to hear me over the noise of the crowd, especially if he had his hearing aid turned off, but the gesture would surely be noticed.

But he ignored me and made a beeline for the mayor, who was doing some pointing and gesturing of his own, ordering the next crew to work. I jumped down off the stage and followed my own beeline, hoping to cut him off before he reached the mayor.

"Sheriff!"

Sheriff Mercer, with Sheriff Locke in tow, seemed intent on connecting with Mayor Ellington. I intercepted him only a couple of yards before he reached his intended victim.

"Sheriff! I have to talk to you—"

"Not now, C.W." He brushed me aside and caught up with the mayor in a few quick steps. I was right behind him.

"But, Sheriff—" My words fell on deaf ears, so to speak. I wasn't referring to his recently acquired hearing accessory.

Sheriff Mercer placed a strong hand on the mayor's shoulder and pulled him aside. I stood nearby and tried to read his lips. Something important was going on.

"Connor—" Sheriff Locke apparently knew what I was up to. She tried to distract me but I held up my hand to shush her and focused on the sheriff's lips.

"Elijah, we got a problem," I saw the sheriff say.

The mayor shook his head and said something. It looked like he was giving the sheriff his own, "Not now." The sheriff didn't take "not now" for an answer. Grabbing Mayor Ellington by both shoulders, Sheriff Mercer looked him in the eye and said, "Listen to me. We got major trouble."

He finally had the mayor's attention. And certainly mine.

Mayor Ellington stood quietly while the sheriff took a deep breath. I watched his lips carefully, not wanting to miss a word. But the shocker didn't come from him. Sheriff Locke was speaking. I nearly missed what she said.

"—and there may not be any opening ceremonies, Mayor. There may not even be a Jubilee."

All this for a dead frog? Things were getting crazy around here.

The mayor began to argue, then shut up when the sheriff gripped his shoulders firmly again. I stepped forward a foot so I could make out exactly what was threatening the famous Jumping Frog Jubilee, my eyes on all three of them. Sheriff Locke began to speak again. Her lips were easy to read, but I wasn't sure I read them right. It looked like she said:

"Dakota Webster is missing."

Chapter 5

"WHAT DO YOU mean, Dakota's missing?" the mayor shot back at Sheriff Locke.

In my efforts to reach the sheriff, I hadn't noticed the two women I'd seen at the diner, Simonie Scott and her older companion. Simonie looked frantic; the other woman seemed mildly irritated.

"Just what she said, Mayor," Simonie interrupted. Mayor Ellington turned his attention to the young nurse, puzzled by this new wrench in the cogs.

"I still don't know what you mean by *missing*. Has he been kidnapped or something? Was there a ransom note? Did a space ship beam him up?" the mayor demanded.

I thought Simonie was going to slap him for excessive sarcasm, but she was just a hand-waver. She emphasized all her words with meaningless gestures. It was distracting for me, to say the least.

"What I mean is," she said slowly, as if the mayor was a child, "I went over to his house to pick him up for the Jubilee—he's been working with his backup frog, you know, since Buford was murdered. And he wasn't there. And neither was his other frog."

"So?" Mayor Ellington replied.

"So!" She looked at Sheriff Mercer. "You know Dakota, Sheriff! He wouldn't quit, just 'cause one of his frogs got whacked."

The sheriff took over. "You're right, Simonie, but that doesn't necessarily mean he's missing. He probably came here early to check in and get ready. In fact, didn't I see the two of you a while ago, over at the training grounds?"

"That was hours ago. And he couldn't have come here by himself!" Simonie protested. Her body language showed concern, but not the kind I expected. She seemed more angry than upset that he might be missing. "His car is in the shop. I was supposed to pick him up."

The sheriff checked his watch. Ten minutes to go. As champion frog jockey five years running, Dakota was slated to be a part of the welcoming ceremonies. He'd become a sort of celebrity in the Mother Lode country over the last few years.

"Well, hold tight. He may show up. I can't put out a missing persons until he's been gone forty-eight hours. I'm sure he'll be here."

The woman in the suit spoke up for the first time. I glanced at her nameplate: JANET MACAVITY, BUSINESS DEPARTMENT. She looked the type—dry, stiff, businesslike. Her hair was too short, her skirt was too long, and her arms were tightly crossed in front of her chest.

"Sheriff, I think you're making a big mistake. If something has happened to Dakota Webster, it could be devastating for the Jubilee, not to mention Dakota himself. I hope you're not forgetting that someone killed his frog. And maybe that someone had a reason—"

"Excuse me, but who are you?" Mayor Ellington interrupted. The conversation was becoming more and more difficult to follow with all the different mouths moving practically at the same time. I felt like a loose racquetball bouncing off four walls.

"I'm Janet Macavity, a friend of Simonie's."

Sheriff Mercer glanced down at her hospital nameplate, but he must not have read it. "You a doctor?"

"No. I'm the business manager at Mother Lode Memorial. I'm also on the Jubilee committee. Our hospital benefits from this event, and I'd hate to see the festivities cancelled. But we've got a real situation here."

I looked the woman over. What was her angle? If the event were cancelled, the hospital would lose a tremendous amount of money. Was she Simonie's mother? Or Dakota's? Different last names meant nothing these days.

"If something bad has happened to Dakota and one of the attendees finds him before the police do, it could cause pandemonium," Janet continued. "It might be a good idea just to delay the opening for a while. That way you can make a thorough search before word spreads."

"Thank you for your advice," the sheriff said, impatiently dismissing her. "But until—"

All heads turned to look behind me. I whirled around to see what had suddenly attracted their attention.

It was the nurse who had thrown punch on Simonie at the Nugget. She, too, had a nameplate: HOLLY SAMUELS. I caught her somewhere in the middle of her words. "...has happened to him and it's her fault. She's the one—"

Before Holly could say anything more, Simonie pushed through the gathering crowd and slapped Holly. Momentarily stunned, Holly dove after her in retaliation and fell, pulling Simonie down with her. The two tussled in the sawdust, grabbing at one another's uniforms, scratching, pulling hair. It took the sheriff and the mayor to pry the women apart. While Sheriff Mercer grabbed hold of Holly's arm and hoisted her up, Mayor Ellington pulled on Simonie. Sheriff Locke stood nearby ready for crowd control.

With one hand Sheriff Mercer brushed the dust from his normally impeccable uniform. He kept a firm hold on Holly with the other. "What the hell is going on here?"

"Ask *her!*" Holly said, pointing to Simonie, her face contorted. I had a feeling she was yelling.

I looked at Simonie and Holly, both nurses, both young and attractive, and wondered if there was some kind of romantic triangle among the two women and Dakota Webster. Love always seemed to stimulate passion like this. But how did Janet Macavity fit in?

"Look, I don't know what all this is about," Mayor Ellington said, "but I think we better go on with the opening ceremony as planned. All hell's going to break loose if we cancel at this point."

Sheriff Mercer nodded reluctantly. "Until I have some kind of evidence that Dakota is in real trouble, I guess we can't disappoint all these people who paid good money to come to the Jubilee."

"Besides," Sheriff Locke added, "while they're distracted with the festivities, Elvis and I can have a look around."

"You're worried about a scandal, aren't you!" spat Simonie at the mayor. "Don't you realize someone's life is at stake?"

"You're the one who's gotten him into all this trouble," Holly spat back.

"Trouble! You're the one who is in *trouble*," Simonie countered. "You just can't stand the fact that he wants me and not you."

"He doesn't want you! He's using you, just like he uses everyone else," Holly screamed.

She turned to go, but stepped into a hole in the ground, and twisted her ankle. I was standing nearby and caught her by the elbow before she hit the ground. She didn't even thank me. She mumbled a few words I couldn't make out as she straightened her nurse's smock, then looked me in the eye and said something like "...farmers see..." Finally she stomped away.

"What was that all about?" I asked Simonie. She ignored me.

"Bitch," was all she said, mostly to herself.

"Look, Simonie," Sheriff Mercer said. "We don't have much to go on here. What makes you think Dakota might really be in trouble and not just hiding out for a while?"

"Sheriff, you know how competitive these guys are. The winner gets a big cash prize. He gets his face in all the papers and on TV. And he's a local. I know some of the jockeys are fed up with Dakota winning year after year. I can name one in particular." She stared pointedly at Sheriff Mercer.

"If you're implying my son Miah had anything to do with this—"

Simonie cut him off. "I'm saying there are lots of people who would like to see Dakota out of the way. But he doesn't quit so easily. He had another frog he was sure would be a winner, too. Maybe someone is keeping him away from the competition until the deadline's past, so he's disqualified. Ever think of that?"

Simonie had a point. Miah Mercer wasn't the only one who was tired of seeing the egotistical nursing student win five years in a row. I wondered if the possibility that he was being detained warranted some thought. If killing his champion frog wasn't enough to keep Dakota out of the competition, maybe some disgruntled loser had decided to take it to the next level and make certain he'd miss the cut-off time.

Sheriff Mercer checked his watch once more. We were at the wire; it was showtime in Frogtown. But would the show go on?

"All right, all right. Let's delay it half an hour. Then we'll start it up, whether we find him or not."

"But...but...Sheriff!" the mayor sputtered. "You can't delay the opening! The crowd will riot! Have you ever seen frog fanatics when they're upset? It'll be chaos—"

"It's just half an hour, Elijah," Sheriff Locke said, backing him up. "Most of these people will be three sheets to the wind by then with all the beer around here. They won't even notice. Just make a short announcement over the PA and tell everyone we've got some kind of technical difficulty and have to delay the ceremony for thirty minutes."

"But...but—"

I thought I saw steam coming out of the mayor's ears, just like in the cartoons on TV, but it could have been my imagination. In any case, the mayor said nothing—at least out loud.

He said plenty with his body language. With a last glare first at Sheriff Locke, then at Sheriff Mercer, he turned and stomped off. There was a lot of stomping going around.

While the mayor headed for the stage to make an announcement about the delay, someone tapped me on the shoulder.

"Dan!" In all the commotion, I'd forgotten about him.

"I've been looking all over for you. What's up? What kind of technical problems?" He held a green sno-cone in one hand and a green-battered corn dog in the other. Must not have been looking for me too hard.

It took me a minute to realize what Dan was talking about.

He nodded to the mayor. "The announcement? What's up with that? The mayor wouldn't delay the opening without a really good reason." Dan took a bite of the corn dog, followed by a bite of the sno-cone. Once that was completed, he offered the junk food to me. I shook my head. The thought of a corn dog washed down with a sno-cone—especially green— made me want to puke.

"Seems your client is lost."

I think Dan swallowed the rest of his mouthful whole. He nearly choked. "What do you mean?" I think he said.

"Simonie Scott went by to pick him up for the opening ceremonies, and he wasn't there. She thinks he's been kidnapped or is being held against his will or something, so he can't participate in the contest."

Dan made a "no shit?" face. "Sheriff on it?"

I nodded. "I think I'll have a look around, too. Sheriff wants us to be discreet, and we only have thirty minutes to make a quick search. There's nothing else to do at this point."

Dan looked dubious, then gave a what-the-hell shrug. "I'll join you." He finished off the corn dog in one big bite, pulling the stick from his mouth as if he were a magician who'd just completed an amazing disappearing act.

I spotted Del Rey and her sister near the stage stairs, looking confused. "Just a sec. I'll be right back."

I headed over, waving at the two nearly identical women. Only one waved back—Del Rey. It was weird seeing my friend's face on two bodies. Especially one that didn't respond.

"Connor! What happened?" Del Rey asked. "I just heard the announcement. What's the delay?" Del Ores turned in my general direction, a practiced smile on her face. I wondered if she'd been taught to keep a pleasant look on her face for the sake of seeing people?

"Hi, Del Rey. Hi, Del Ores. Glad you could make it." I reached out and this time gently touched Del Ores in greeting. The touch didn't seem to make her wince as much as the first time. I'd heard that blind people are "tactilely defensive" but had forgotten that when I touched her shoulder earlier. This time I was more careful.

"I'm not supposed to say anything...." I made a concerted effort to lower my voice but I could never be sure I was successful. "One of the contestants in the frog-jumping competition—Dakota Webster—he's apparently missing. Or so his girlfriend thinks. The sheriff is making a quick search before beginning the festivities. It should only be about a half an hour delay."

"Wow! I wonder what happened to him." Del Rey checked her watch. "Well, I suppose we could get something to eat. Shall we meet you back here about 7:25?"

I nodded, then for the sake of Del Ores said, "Yes, that would be fine. I'm going to take a look around myself, but I'll be back by then."

I watched Del Rey nudge her elbow gently into Del Ores's side. I had expected Del Rey to take her sister's arm and lead her, as I would have been tempted to do, but instead Del Ores took Del Rey's arm, grasping it lightly from behind, and followed Del Rey into the crowd. I realized I had a lot to learn about blindness.

I joined Dan and we headed for the frog-jumping arena, the most likely place to start a search for a contestant. There were lots of little kids goosing their frogs, calling them by silly names, slapping the ground to get their jumpers to jump. But no sign of Dakota.

While Dan questioned some of the other entrants, I watched the young trainers try to coerce their frogs into jumping in a straight line. Most of the contestants were hopping all over the place—sideways, backwards, even zigzagging. They looked pretty hopeless to me. I wondered how Dakota had managed to win the event year after year. Did he have some kind of secret strategy?

I asked a few of the dressed-up cowboys on the staff if they might know where Dakota did his training. One Buffalo Bill look-alike said he didn't know anything about that, but he thought he saw a guy who looked like Dakota headed toward the creek, "yonder." I thanked him, then went to meet Dan at the arena gate.

"Anything?" I asked.

"Someone saw him a couple of hours ago. Over near Critter's Creek."

"I got the same info. What was he doing there? Searching for more winners?"

"Seems a little late for that," said Dan. "But we better check it out."

I followed Dan to the rear of the fairgrounds and out the back exit marked NO ADMITTANCE. The grounds were surrounded by a high chain-link fence, separating the area from the creek. Naturally kids had worked a hole in the fence so they could get to the water. It was just big enough for an adult to climb through, although not without catching some clothing on a few of the jutting wires.

"Damn it! I tore my shirt!" I pulled at the T-shirt that featured the Budweiser frogs across the front. Miah had designed it by scanning the frogs onto the shirt and adding his own caption: THE EUREKA'S WORST VERSE CONTEST.

Dan looked back and grinned at the hole in my shirt, located right in the middle of my left breast. Good thing I was wearing my yellow bra. It looked as if one of the frogs had a pointy yellow forehead.

"Come on. But be careful, it's slippery along the edge."

Critter's Creek was a favorite play area for kids and apparently a fun party area for the teenagers. Beer cans lay discarded along the creek bed, as well as cigarette butts, candy wrappers, condoms, and even a pair of bikini underpants. Dan and I hiked along the water's edge to an area that was famous for its frogs.

Manzanita bushes grew full on the other side of the creek, leading to a thick forest of pine trees and eucalyptus. A wide pool in the middle of the creek made a frog pond, dotted with large smooth stones, water moss, lily pads, and cattails. The stones created a perfect bridge to the other side of the creek.

Like a tightrope walker, I followed Dan across the two-foot depth, just managing to keep from stepping in the water and ruining my Doc Martens. Due to my hearing loss, I don't have a great sense of balance, but my desire to keep my good shoes dry helped compensate for my disability.

"Look here," Dan said, when we reached the other side. He had knelt down and was pointing to something in the water. I saw no movement, and it took me a moment to recognize what was camouflaged by moss and reeds.

Tiny frogs. Washed up to the edge of the creek, not moving. Floaters.

"They're all dead!" I said, pulling back in horror. I hate to see any kind of animal threatened or in distress. I especially like frogs because they are cute and eat flies. Someone told me they make an interesting noise, too. It was described as sounding like the word "ribbet" but that didn't help much. How can a frog say "ribbet"?

"Yeah. That's weird." Dan stood up and scanned the area. As he moved down the creek, he checked the water now and then for more dead frogs. Then something moved out from under a large, thick bush that overhung the water.

"Shit! A snake!" he said, pulling back from the bush. He held a hand back to keep me from getting closer.

I think I screamed. "Is it poisonous?"

"I don't know. Want me to check?" He gave me a sarcastic look. I gave him a dirty look. The snake slithered into the water and disappeared. I moved over close to Dan, glancing at the bush where the snake had first appeared.

"Any more in there?" I asked.

Dan picked up a stick and stuck it into the bush. He wiggled it around but nothing came slithering out. "Doesn't look like—"

Dan stopped. The stick, still in the bush, froze in his grasp.

"Oh God," he said. His words and expression sent a chill up my spine.

"More dead frogs? Or more snakes?" I pulled back.

He shook his head. Slowly he lifted up the lowest branch of the bush with the stick.

A human hand floated in the muddy water.

When I realized it was connected to an arm that disappeared into the overgrown bushes, I screamed again.

Chapter 6

SEEING DEAD BODIES makes me puke. The last time I stumbled on one, I hurled big-time. This one was no different.

When I finished spewing my dinner, I caught a glimpse of Dan waving his arms in my peripheral vision and looked up.

"Watch it!" he said. "This is a crime scene."

"Hey, I'm sick here," I snapped back, wiping the drool from my mouth. "A little consideration for the still-living would be nice."

"Sorry," he said sheepishly. "Old cop reflex. I just didn't want you to disturb the scene."

"It's Dakota, isn't it?" I asked, stealing a quick glance at the body. I can't say I recognized him, face-down in the muddy water, but I recognized the hospital greens.

Dan nodded. "Looks like he drowned." As much as I feared the inevitable nightmares, I found myself unable to look away from the grisly scene. Kind of like passing a car accident.

"I think he—" Dan stopped abruptly and raised a hand, alert to something downstream. I froze.

Was someone hiding nearby?

Dan moved slowly back from the edge of the creek, his hand on the bulge at his chest. As a newly licensed P.I., Dan had a permit to carry a gun. I forgot about it most of the time. Until we started making out.

I stood still, my heart pounding a drumbeat. I wondered if it was loud enough to hear outside of my chest.

Dan inched down the creek bed and focused on another large bush several yards away. I strained to see what had caught his attention and noticed a sudden movement in the thick underbrush.

An animal? I hoped and prayed.

I couldn't hear what was going on, but Dan's body language was loud and clear. He took a defensive stance, feet apart, arms straight, his gun pointing directly into the bush. After a second, he started to say something I couldn't read from that angle. I had a feeling he was calling for the hidden figure to reveal itself.

And then, to my surprise, I actually heard something.

A blast, accompanied by a flash of bright light. The loud noise felt like a rock striking my chest. I slapped my hands over my ears and looked for the source, disoriented. Dan stood holding his gun aimed straight up in the air.

He must have fired a warning shot. And I had heard the explosion of the gun as it went off. I could feel my heart racing double-time.

Two hands immediately stuck up out of the bushes. Dan waved his gun and said something else I couldn't read. Out stepped a tall figure, arms up, the long fingers of his hands trembling, legs covered in mud from the knees of the jeans to the once-white athletic shoes.

"Miah!" I yelled, startling Dan as I lunged past him. Dan lowered the gun and shook his head. "Dan, you almost shot Miah!"

"Jesus Christ, Miah! What the fuck are you doing hiding in these bushes!" Dan looked more angry than relieved to find it was someone he knew—and that he hadn't shot him. I couldn't blame him for being upset. He could have killed Miah by accident if he hadn't been so cautious.

Miah said nothing but looked from Dan's glowering eyes to my puzzled ones.

"Miah?" I said again, gently this time. "What are you doing here?"

Dan must have had the same thought I had. We locked eyes, then stared at Miah.

"I...I know what you're thinking...but I didn't do it—"

Miah never got to finish his plea. A throng of mostly men—Sheriff Mercer's makeshift posse—appeared from both directions of the creek. A few steps behind the sheriff came Simonie and her friend Janet. Beyond them, I could see rubberneckers gawking through the fairground fence. They all must have heard the gunshot. And this was probably a lot more interesting than a few jumping frogs and a green corn dog.

Simonie took one look at the scene—first Miah standing there with his hands still up in the air, then the body bobbing in the gentle ripple of the creek water—and for the second time that day, I heard a sound. This time it was Simonie's high-pitched scream. I can hear very high and very low sounds—bat cries, motorcycle rumbles—it's the noises in between I have trouble with.

Janet Macavity rushed to her side and held her, but Simonie would have none of her comforting.

"You killed him! I knew it!" Simonie screamed at Miah. I couldn't hear her words, but I could lip-read her well enough even though her face was twisted with anger and grief. "You've hated him since high school, and you've always been jealous of him! And now you've killed him. Well, Jeremiah Mercer, you're not going to get away with it!"

Simonie lunged for Miah but Dan intercepted her, restraining her by the shoulders. She broke into hysterical sobs. I turned to Sheriff Mercer. For the first time since I'd known him he looked helpless. He stood staring at his son, speechless, his brow deeply furrowed. I'd never seen the sheriff at a loss for words before.

"Dad—" Miah stepped forward. The mud sucked at his shoes, making it difficult for him to walk. He tried stepping on a large smooth stone and nearly lost his balance. "Dad, I swear. I found him here, just lying in the creek. I tried to get him out but—"

"You liar!" Simonie was back in full swing. Dan kept her locked in his tight grip as she flailed her arms. Once she'd calmed down again, she looked spent. She spat out, "Sheriff, arrest this lying bastard or I'll do it myself."

"Let's all relax, now," Sheriff Mercer said. "Ms. Macavity, I want you to take Ms. Scott back to the fairgrounds, find the medical tent, and get her something to calm her down, you hear?"

Janet nodded, and began leading Simonie away. Simonie turned back for one more jab. I missed her words, but I caught Miah's expression—he looked pained and shaken.

The sheriff continued giving orders. "Miah, you come with me. I need to ask you a few questions."

Miah said nothing. I thought I caught a glimmer of tears in his eyes, but he blinked them back and headed over to his father.

"Peyton," Sheriff Mercer turned to Sheriff Locke. "Would you call the coroner and get her out here, ASAP," the sheriff said. "And keep an eye on the scene. I don't want anyone fooling with it—any more than they already have." Sheriff Mercer shot me a look, then turned to address the curious crowd. Apparently death was the ultimate entertainment. "Show's over, folks. Thanks for your help. Now you can do us all a favor by going back to the Jubilee."

The Jubilee? Surely it would be cancelled now that a body had been found.

As the crowd slowly dispersed, I spotted a woman standing on the periphery of the activity. Holly Samuels, the nurse who had poured punch on Simonie Scott. She seemed mesmerized by the sight of Dakota's body. Her face showed no emotion until she caught me watching her. Then she sucked in her lips, frowned, and turned away. She was gone before I could ask her anything about the death of Dakota Webster.

Instead of following Sheriff Mercer and Miah back to the
police tent, Dan and I waited for Arthurlene Jackson, the
chief medical examiner for Calaveras County. Arthurlene
pulled up in a county car and stepped out, looking more like
a model for *Ebony* than a medical examiner. She shook her
head with its tiny black curls when she spotted me. She always did that. It wasn't that Arthurlene didn't like me. It's just
that she thought I got in her way at times, which of course
wasn't true.

"Connor Westphal. Surprise, surprise." I had a feeling she
was being sarcastic.

"Hi, Dr. Jackson. How's it going?"

"Good until now. What's your part in all this? I suppose you
found the body?"

Before I could answer, Sheriff Peyton Locke headed over
to greet Arthurlene. She filled in the M.E. while I made myself invisible in the background. I wanted to look around before the scene got cold—and they'd be kicking me out any
moment. I decided to keep a low profile and check out the
area farther downstream, where Miah had been...hiding?

Stepping carefully and keeping to moss and rocks, I
headed back to the point where Dan had discovered Miah.
Manzanita bushes grew abundant and dense in this area,
thanks to the widening of the creek. The shrubbery was a little
prickly but still good for hiding.

I bent over and bear-crawled inside through a small opening, scanning the ground for anything that might belong to
Miah—or Dakota. I found a dried snakeskin that made me
shudder and a couple of squashed beer cans that seemed to
be more indigenous than evergreens in these parts. Cigarette
butts. Condoms. Last year's frog hat, faded and decaying.
One new athletic shoe, size 12, expensive-looking, now home
to a fuzzy caterpillar. A gas can, rusted and dented. A pill
bottle, unlabeled.

The sheriffs would want to check out this area. I didn't
touch anything—I knew the rules—but I was especially inter-

ested in the new shoe. It obviously hadn't been there long. Dakota's? I hadn't noticed earlier whether he was wearing both shoes, too stunned by the discovery of his body. I made a mental note to check.

I crawled out of the bushes and stepped back toward the creek to see if anything unusual was floating in the water. Squatting down, I felt the cool breeze off the water, and took in the smell of moss, damp earth, and that peculiar aroma you only find at creeks. I'd spent a lot of time playing alone in a nearby creek as a kid, studying those water spiders with the big feet that walk on the surface of the water, catching newts and tadpoles, trying to skip rocks. Good memories, now fogged by the discovery of Dakota's body.

Opening my clenched hand, I let my fingers dangle in the slowly moving water and felt the cool massage of the trickling stream. After a few seconds of soothing calm, something caught in my hand. Something slimy. Reflexively I shook my hand free, sprinkling water over my face and arms.

I looked down at what had dropped from my hand. Another frog, now floating in the gentle motion of the water.

Dead.

I stood up. Scanning the edge of the creek bed, I saw them. Hundreds of them. Tiny brownish-green lumps, some caught in the moss, some washed up on the bank, some floating down Critter's Creek.

My stomach pitched at the sight.

What was killing the frogs of Calaveras County?

"Find anything?" I called out to Arthurlene as I approached her. She had just stood up from examining the body and was removing the white surgical gloves from her mahogany-colored hands. Sheriff Peyton Locke stood at attention, guarding the scene. I recognized two young skateboarders, Matt and Brian, peeking through the fairgrounds fence, trying to get a look. Sheriff Locke waved them away to no avail.

"Won't know until I do an autopsy," Arthurlene said. "The creek is awfully shallow here, but he still could have drowned."

"You mean he could have slipped and hit his head?" I asked.

Arthurlene shook her curls. "No head injuries. I doubt if it was an accident, but I haven't found any signs of foul play yet. Superficially, there's not a mark on the body." She paused, then met my eyes. "I don't suppose you have any idea what happened, Connor?"

Arthurlene Jackson always thought I knew more than I did. I think she half suspected me in many of the cases she worked on.

I gave an exaggerated shrug. "How would I know? I'm not a coroner."

"Neither am I. I'm a medical examiner."

"Whatever. And I'm not a detective. I don't have any idea what happened. But I do know this—Jeremiah Mercer had nothing to do with it."

Arthurlene Jackson glanced at Sheriff Locke, who shrugged. "Somebody saying he did?"

"As a matter of fact, yes," I said. "Somebody's actually claiming Miah killed Dakota. I sure hope you can prove that wrong when you do your autopsy."

Arthurlene Jackson said nothing, but Sheriff Locke's pale face flushed. She appeared uncomfortable. After all, we were discussing her boyfriend's son. While Arthurlene packed up her briefcase and bag, the sheriff signaled the paramedics, who had just arrived.

Remembering the shoe, I glanced over at the body and checked the feet. One shoe was missing. I had a feeling I knew where the other one was.

"Sheriff, you might want to check that area down there," I pointed into the manzanita. "I thought I saw a shoe that might belong to Dakota Webster."

The sheriff nodded. The medical examiner headed for her car and I followed her.

"Dr. Jackson, did you find anything that might give us some idea what happened to him?"

Arthurlene got in the car, then faced me through the window. I squatted to read her lips more easily. "Someone's really accusing Sheriff Mercer's son?"

I nodded.

"God, I'd hate to see something happen to his kid if he didn't deserve it. The sheriff's a great guy." She paused, then turned to her briefcase lying on the seat next to her, opened it, and pulled out a plastic bag. She held it up at the window for me to see.

"A frog?" I said, stating the obvious. "I found a bunch of them downstream. All dead."

Arthurlene frowned. "Well, it looks like this one didn't die of natural causes."

"I'm not sure the other frogs did either."

"But this one I can prove. It was poked through the stomach with something sharp."

I winced, then took the bag from Dr. Jackson's hand, held it up, and stared at the frog. "This one is a lot bigger than the little frogs floating in the creek."

I turned it over—and froze. This one had a dot of red on the abdomen, about the size of a baby's fingernail. I knew it was nail polish.

"Where did you find it?" I managed to ask.

"You sure you want to know?"

I nodded.

"In Dakota's mouth."

"Oh, my God!" I gasped in horror. Talk about a frog in your throat. But it wasn't the thought of the frog in the dead man's mouth that caused the blood to leave my head.

I recognized that frog. And I knew who had painted that dot of nail polish on the abdomen, just like he did every year. It was his signature.

Miah.

Chapter 7

I SAID NOTHING about the red dot to Arthurlene as I handed over the frog. In fact, I said nothing at all. I just gave her a weak smile and stepped back so she could drive away.

A few dozen panicky thoughts ran through my disheveled brain. I settled on one. I had to talk with Miah. Sooner or later someone would figure out whose frog sported a red dot on its tummy. And that wouldn't look good for Miah.

As I headed back for the fairgrounds, I wondered whether the Jubilee had been postponed or called off, now that Dakota's body had been found. I knew Mayor Ellington. He'd do everything in his power to convince the board to keep the festival going—and to cover up the discovery of the body. But as publisher of my own newspaper, it was my job to let people know what happened. After all, someone had murdered Dakota Webster and whoever it was, was still loose. 'Cause it sure wasn't Miah.

I hustled through the opening in the fence and immediately had my answer about the fate of the Jubilee. The crowd had thinned considerably, and those who remained looked mighty disappointed, verging on angry.

I headed for the stage where I'd promised to meet Del Rey and Del Ores. They stood nearby, Del Rey holding an ice cream cone, Del Ores with a soda and straw.

"Del Rey! You're still here! I'm sorry I kept you both waiting."

Del Ores turned in the direction of my voice. Del Rey held

up her cone as though she were the Statue of Liberty. "Hey, Connor. About time."

"I'm so sorry I'm late!" I said again. I reached out to touch Del Ores's arm but restrained myself remembering her discomfort. "I suppose you heard what happened?"

"Only what was announced over the loudspeaker—that there was some kind of accident," Del Ores said in my general direction.

"Accident, huh. That's an understatement," I replied. "Anything else?"

"No, but there are a lot of rumors flying around. So what happened? Someone's frog get a leg cramp or what?" Del Rey licked her cone. Nothing came between Del Rey and her dairy products.

I pulled the sisters away from a couple of bystanders, not knowing how far my voice would carry. I'm not always good at monitoring the volume, and I didn't want to take any chances someone might overhear what I had to share.

"What did the mayor say exactly?" I said as softly as I could.

"Nothing much," Del Rey said. "About fifteen minutes ago he got up on the stage and told everyone there'd been an accident and the opening ceremonies would be postponed until tomorrow morning."

"That's it?"

"When people in the crowd started yelling at him, demanding to know what happened, he said he'd explain it all tomorrow morning. Then he got the hell off the stage. I think he just said that so they'd all come back tomorrow to find out the details. You know how everyone loves small-town gossip."

I did. That's why my newspaper had been growing in circulation. "So the Jubilee isn't cancelled completely?"

"Apparently not. Why? Was it something serious?" Del Rey asked.

Del Ores added, "We've been hearing all kinds of whispered speculation. The rumors are spreading through the crowd like a—"

"A case of viral warts," I interrupted, remembering one of the Worst Verse entries.

Del Ores broke into a broad grin. "Good one."

"So what did you hear?" I asked.

"The guy next to me said something about a body that was found lying at the bottom of the creek," Del Ores said. "Another guy said he heard it was two bodies, both stabbed. Someone else claimed the dead guy was floating down the creek and his eyes were pecked out by birds. I quit listening after that."

"It's a good thing you publish a newspaper, Connor," Del Rey said. "If we left it to the grapevine, Mayor Ellington would be floating down the Nile on the back of a mutant Frogzilla."

"Well, there was a body found. In Critter's Creek."

"Oh, God!" Del Rey slapped her hand over her mouth. She removed it just enough to ask, "Who was it?"

"Dakota Webster."

"Oh, my God!" The hand went back over the mouth. But not for long. "What happened? Was he...murdered?"

"The medical examiner doesn't think it was an accident. I'm sure she suspects foul play but can't confirm anything until she's done an autopsy. Of course, maybe he committed suicide by shoving his head under water."

Del Ores grimaced. Del Rey's eyes nearly bulged out of her head. "Who...did they catch the guy who did it?"

I didn't exactly know how to answer that one. "They're questioning someone. But—"

"Who is it?" Del Rey demanded.

I hesitated, but I knew I had to tell her. She'd find out sooner or later, and I wanted to be the one to let her know. After all, Miah and Del Rey's son Andrew had become good friends since Andrew returned from college. They'd even gone into the beer-making business together.

"Miah."

After promising to fill in a stunned Del Rey with any pertinent news, I said good-bye. We agreed to meet first thing in the morning, when I hoped I'd finally get to announce the Worst Verse winner. Then I rushed off to find out why Miah had been at the creek.

I found him at the sheriff's office, sitting in the same chair he'd occupied earlier, looking even more forlorn.

"Miah!"

"Hey, C.W.," Sheriff Mercer answered instead. He looked almost as lost as his son. "Figured you'd show up eventually. Learn anything more from Arthurlene?"

I thought about the red-dotted frog and decided to hold back until I learned why Miah had been at the creek.

"Nothing much." I headed over to Miah and pulled up a chair next to him. I patted his knee a few times, trying to ease into the interrogation. "How're you doing, Miah?"

He said nothing, nor did he move. He just kept his eyes on his long legs stretched out in front of him.

I faced the sheriff. "Sheriff, could I talk with Miah for a few minutes?"

Sheriff Mercer frowned. Those deepening lines in his forehead would never fade. Finally he stood, tucked in the back of his shirt, and headed for the door. "I could use a cup of java. Want one of those mochas you're always drinking?"

I shook my head.

"Be back in five." With a last glance at his son, Sheriff Mercer shut the door behind him. I turned my attention to his son.

"Miah, what were you doing at the creek?" Because it was Miah, I found myself using sign language out of habit.

He shot me a look and said out loud, "I don't feel like signing right now, Connor. Okay?"

I dropped the signs and continued verbally. "Miah, I know you didn't kill Dakota. But you must have had a reason for being at Critter's Creek."

He said nothing.

"Did you find the body?"

For the first time Miah met my eyes. Tears rimmed the edges of his lids. He blinked several times, restraining the flow.

"Tell me about it."

He took a deep breath before answering, then said, "I've already told my dad. I went down there because I got a note to meet him there—"

"A note to meet Dakota at Critter's Creek?"

Miah nodded. "It said if I didn't come, he'd make sure I was disqualified for the jump. I wasn't going to go, but I figured he was up to something and I wanted to find out what it was. God, I can't believe we used to be such good friends. He was such a jerk after he started..."

Miah shifted his gaze to the window.

"What, Miah? After he started what?"

"He just changed, that's all."

"After Simonie?"

Miah's eyes tightened. "Once the two of them got together, it was like their personalities changed. They started drinking all the time. After Dakota got into nursing school, every time I saw him it seemed like he was either on speed to keep up the pace, or he was toking up to wind down. I mean, I'm no saint, but he really went off the deep end."

"So you got a note from him and you went to the creek to meet him? When?"

"About an hour before the opening ceremonies were to begin."

"Did you find him there right away?"

"Not at first. He wasn't where he said he'd be. I hung around awhile, waiting for him. When he didn't show after about half an hour, I figured I'd walk upstream a bit and see if I'd missed him, then head back to the fairgrounds. It was almost starting time. I thought maybe he was trying to keep me from being there or something. Anyway, that's when..." He paused, a far-off look in his eyes.

"You found him?"

Tears relined Miah's eyes. "I saw this arm sticking out of

the water. I thought it was a joke. I thought he wanted to scare me or something with a fake arm floating in the water. But when I poked it with a stick, I saw the rest of him...."

Miah dropped his head in his hand. I couldn't see his face, but I knew he was crying. I'd never seen him cry, and I felt for him. I waited a few moments before continuing.

"Was he already...dead?"

Miah nodded, his head still in his hand.

"What did you do then?" I thought about the red-dotted frog.

"Nothing! I heard someone coming and panicked. I didn't know who it was, so I jumped into the bushes. I was afraid they'd see me if I tried to run off."

"Why didn't you come out when you knew it was us?"

"I don't know. I was scared. I was afraid you'd think..."

I patted his knee again. "Miah, that's ridiculous. I don't care what anyone says, you'd never kill anyone or anything." I thought again about his frog. "Your dad and Dan and I will do everything we can to help you and find out who killed Dakota. But you have to help."

He looked up, his eyes red, his cheeks damp. He wiped away the tears with his jacket sleeve.

"I have one more question. Where's your frog?"

He didn't seem to process the question at first. "What do you mean?"

"Your frog. Freddy. Where is he?"

"At my comic book shop in his little swimming pool, where he always is. Why?" Miah suddenly paled, looking frantic. "Has something happened to him?"

I sat up. "I think so."

"What do you mean?" He leaped from his chair and headed for the door. I raced him there and blocked his exit.

"Wait. I have something to tell you."

Miah paused.

"Freddy was...found at the scene. By Dr. Jackson."

"What...what was he doing there? Did Dakota have him?"

"I don't know. But I have a feeling you're going to be asked that question yourself, so be prepared."

"Where is he now?" Miah grabbed the doorknob. I pulled him back around.

"Miah, calm down. Dr. Jackson has your frog."

"What's she doing with him? I want him back. I'm not dropping out of this contest, no matter what Dakota tried to—"

"Miah, Freddy is dead."

Miah stiffened. I could see a mixture of horror and rage fill his face. "What do you mean, he's dead?" he said slowly, controlled.

"Dr. Jackson found him on Dakota's body."

"Shit! Dakota killed him! He thought I killed his frog so he kidnapped my frog and killed him to get even! That son of a—"

Miah stopped. He seemed to suddenly remember his fiercest competitor was dead.

"So Dr. Jackson found my frog on Dakota's body, and now she probably thinks I had something to do with his death," Miah said.

I shrugged. "I don't—"

Miah shook his head. "This is totally fucked," he said to himself, then to me he said, "Are you sure it's Freddy?"

"He had a red dot on his tummy."

Miah frowned. "How did he die?"

"He...drowned."

"Not Dakota. Freddy. How did Freddy die?"

"I don't know. Probably suffocation."

"What do you mean? Frogs don't drown, do they?"

"He didn't drown. He was...stuffed in Dakota's mouth."

Just as Miah ran for the bathroom, Simonie Scott burst through the door. She looked as if she was about to murder someone.

Chapter 8

"WHERE IS HE?"

Simonie Scott stood in the open doorway, looking as if she might kill the first person she saw. That would be me, since Miah was no longer in the room. Before I could respond—or take cover—Janet Macavity stepped in and grabbed her by the shoulders.

"Simonie! You've got to stop this! Let the sheriff do his job." At least that's what I think Janet said. She was turned sideways, and her lips were not easy to read.

Simonie shrugged her off and stepped forward to face me, up close and personal. "He's here, isn't he? Well, he'd better be locked up!"

I didn't have to answer that question either. Miah emerged from the tiny bathroom, wiping his mouth with his sleeve. He froze the moment he saw Simonie.

"Murderer!" she screamed, her face twisted with rage. As she lunged for Miah, he put his arms up to protect himself. It took both Janet and me to pull her off Miah. Simonie managed to gouge his cheek with her perfect nails before we could contain her.

I felt a rush of air and a sudden vibration. The slamming of a door. I caught Sheriff Mercer mid-sentence.

"...the hell is going on here?"

"Why isn't he in jail?" Simonie demanded, pointing a lethal-looking fingernail in Miah's direction.

The sheriff adjusted his gun belt in an obvious gesture of male posturing. "Because he hasn't been charged with anything, that's why."

"But he murdered Dakota! First he killed his frog. And when that wasn't enough to stop him, he killed Dakota. Are you blind? Why can't you see that?"

Janet Macavity tried to hold onto Simonie while she raged, but she couldn't calm her down. Miah had backed up against the wall as Simonie continued her tirade.

"What is it you need, Sheriff? Proof? You've got your proof! He was found only a few feet away from Dakota's body. Pretty convenient, wouldn't you say? He has the strength to drown him. And he obviously had a reason. But you're not going to arrest him, are you? 'Cause he's your son!"

Sheriff Mercer held up his hands to try to calm Simonie. Tears streamed down her face, and her nose was running.

Not one to keep quiet for long, I spoke up. "Simonie, the sheriff is doing everything he can to find out what happened to Dakota. So if you're suggesting—"

"Who the fuck are you?" She directed her rage at me, and for a moment I wanted to flatten myself against the wall, too.

"I'm Connor Westphal. Miah works for me at the *Eureka!*."

"Are you deaf? I'm not *suggesting* anything. I'm saying it like it is. He murdered my boyfriend in cold blood. Now I'm *suggesting* that you mind your own fucking business."

Such a mouth on that girl, using "fuck" as an adjective, when it clearly was meant to be the ultimate expletive.

"Yes, I'm deaf. And yes, it is my business when it concerns my employee, my friend, and my community. You're in danger of slander, and I suggest—"

"Fuck your suggestions! First of all, you don't know what you're talking about. And second, Miah had every reason in the world to kill Cody, didn't you, Miah?" She turned her vicious look on the young man standing meekly against the wall. "Why don't you tell them, Jeremiah, sweetie? Or do you want me to?"

Miah glanced at me, then his father, then back at Simonie, who continued to glare at him. He finally shrugged.

"I don't know what you're talking about."

A venomous grin spread across Simonie's face. "Sheriff, did you know your son and I used to be—"

"Shut up, Simonie!" Miah lashed out suddenly.

"I know all about it, Miss Scott," the sheriff said. "You and he used to be involved. But—"

Simonie's grin widened. "Involved? How about married?"

For several seconds, nothing in the room moved, except the chill running up my spine.

"Miah?" I asked, certain Simonie must be lying.

"Son?" the sheriff asked.

"Darling?" Simonie mocked, the grin twisting as she folded her arms across her chest.

I turned my attention to Miah. His head was pulled back in disbelief. Or was it horror? I didn't have time to define it clearly. He ran from the office, nearly knocking Simonie to the ground as he pushed past her.

Nobody said anything. Finally the sheriff spoke: "I don't believe you."

"Call the county." Simonie rubbed the shoulder where Miah had bumped her. "They'll verify it."

"But why?" The sheriff fell into his chair. This latest bulletin seemed to take the last remaining wind out of his sails. "Why would you get married? Why wouldn't you tell anyone? Why keep it a secret?"

"We were young, stupid, and horny. And we thought we were in love. What a laugh."

Sheriff Mercer glared at her.

"If you'll remember, Sheriff, you didn't particularly approve of me back then. You didn't think your son should be getting so serious about a girl like me. A girl who drank and smoked dope and loved to party. But you weren't getting along with

Miah so great, were you? Maybe he just didn't feel he could confide in you. Maybe he just needed someone back then."

"So he married *you?*" I said, still not able to comprehend her stunning announcement. "Without telling anyone? It just doesn't make sense."

Simonie pulled out a cigarette. There's no smoking in public buildings in California, but the sheriff didn't seem inclined to enforce the law at the moment. She was also harder to lip-read with smoke coming out of her mouth.

"Yeah, I know what you mean. It's hard to believe now, seven years later. But we thought it was romantic. And we loved having a secret. Especially Miah. He didn't feel like he had any control over his life, with you always telling him what to do."

I glanced at Sheriff Mercer. He was hunched over his desk, rubbing his forehead with his hand so hard, I half expected it to smoke.

"So you got married, just to defy Miah's dad? Just to make some kind of statement?" I asked. Out of the corner of my eye, I saw Janet Macavity squirm. I'd almost forgotten she was there, since until this moment she'd said and done little. What was her role in all this, I wondered.

Simonie shot her a look. Janet shrugged in response.

"Well, you'll probably find out from Miah eventually. We didn't get married just because we were passionately in love."

Oh, God. It suddenly dawned on me. "You were pregnant."

Sheriff Mercer looked up. "You were...pregnant?"

Simonie took a dramatic drag on her cigarette and blew the smoke out sideways. The pause gave us all time to think.

"What happened?" I finally asked, since the sheriff seemed to be at a loss. Was he blaming himself for alienating Miah? Or was he imagining his grandchild?

"I miscarried." She took another drag on her cigarette. I wondered if she'd been smoking then, too. Or lying, I thought uncharitably.

"And the marriage?"

She shrugged. "We had it annulled. We kind of grew apart

after that. He was into his stupid skateboarding shit. Comic books. Surfing. No ocean for hundreds of miles, but my guy wants to be a surfer. God, what was I thinking? He was so immature. Never going anywhere. He wasn't even into partying anymore."

"So you broke up, got an annulment, and started dating Miah's best friend, Dakota?"

Simonie shrugged again. It seemed to be her favorite way of expressing herself. "Yeah, I guess." She looked around for a place to extinguish her cigarette, then opened the door to the bathroom and threw it in the toilet. Classy girl.

"And that's when the friendship between Miah and Dakota started to disintegrate. Because of you," I said.

She shot me a look. "Hey, watch who you're blaming. I've got no control over how a guy feels. So Dakota and I fell in love. Can't blame anyone for that. It just happened."

"But my son didn't take it well." The sheriff spoke up for the first time in several minutes. "And you kind of liked that, didn't you, Simonie?"

"No way! I'm sorry they didn't get along after that. But that's not my fault. Guys are so stupid, fighting over girls. It was over between me and Miah before anything got serious between me and Cody. You can even ask him. That is, if he'll tell you the truth. You didn't even know about our relationship, did you, Sheriff? Didn't know you were going to be a grandpa for a while there, did you? And you don't know for sure if your boy is innocent now, do you?"

God, how I wanted to wipe that smirk off her face.

The sheriff stood, his hands trembling, his face scarlet. I thought he might explode, but he spoke in an even manner, overenunciating his words.

"Thank you for coming by, Miss Scott. I appreciate your... input. I'll call you if I need anything else."

He sat down again and began moving papers around on the desk as if he were suddenly very busy. The two women glanced at each other, then tightened their hold on their purses and headed out the door. Just before Simonie slipped through the opening, she turned to the sheriff for a last word.

"Sheriff, I don't think you really know your son at all. He killed Cody, I'm sure of it. And if you don't have him arrested, I'll call Sheriff Locke and she'll take care of it. You wouldn't want that, now would you?"

I'd had enough of her accusations. "Ms. Scott, the sheriff will find out what happened to Dakota, and without bias. There's no need—"

Simonie turned toward me. "Shut the fuck up! God, for a deaf chick, you sure make a lot of noise."

With that, she slammed the door shut. I felt the burst of air and sudden vibration.

There was a pause before either of us spoke.

"Sheriff, what are you going to do?"

Sheriff Mercer looked a decade older than his sixty years, weary with this new burden.

"I don't know, C.W. I just don't know."

"You do know he couldn't have done this."

He rubbed his short hair, ruining his careful combing job. Strands from all over his head stuck out when he was finished. He looked like a porcupine.

"I know that, C.W. At least, I think I know that. But it appears I don't know a whole hell of a lot about my own son. Married? A kid? Miscarriage? Annulled? And now this? Shit, what's happened to us, C.W.? I love my son. Why wasn't I there when he needed me?"

I felt a wave of empathy for the man. He was just beginning to find happiness again with Peyton Locke, and now this.

"Miah will be okay, Sheriff. You'll find out who really murdered Dakota Webster. It's got to be someone who wants us to believe that Miah did it. The question is why?"

"No, the question is, what other secrets has my son been keeping from me?"

Chapter 9

I NEEDED A BREAK from all the drama. I headed for my office, where I hoped to distract myself with a story on the latest events for tomorrow's issue of the *Eureka!*

Dan wasn't in his office when I passed by, not that I needed that particular distraction. I entered my office, then paused as I was about to unload my backpack onto my desk.

Miah's computer was still on, the screen saver active. Mesmerized by the color and movement, I watched for a few seconds as Woody Woodpecker pecked holes all over the screen. Blinking out of my hypnotic trance, I punched "enter." The pecked holes disintegrated into dust, replaced by a mostly white screen, except for two initials in the center, typed in a large, ornate font:

D.W.

Dakota Webster?

Two lines jutted down from the letters, running at opposite angles, to form a sort of pyramid. Following the forty-five-degree-angle lines, I scrolled down to the point where they ended—in either corner of the screen. Underneath each point, at opposite sides of the screen, Miah had typed the initials:

S.S. and **H.S.**

Doodling on the computer? Miah had a knack for turning his ideas and creations into graphics. I was certain S.S. stood for Simonie Scott. The other, H.S., who—or what—did that represent? I scanned my memory for names that had come up recently and that were associated with Dakota Webster—besides Jeremiah Mercer.

There had been that nurse from the Mother Lode Hospital—Holly. What was her last name? Sutton. Sampson.

Samuels. H.S.

I scrolled down further and saw a horizontal line across the bottom of the screen, underneath the two sets of initials. As I zoomed in, the graphic on the screen reduced to form a triangle. I returned the screen to full size.

What was it supposed to mean? I'd have to ask Miah—when he was in a more talkative mood. I printed out the diagram and pulled the copy from the laser printer. Apparently I hadn't scrolled far enough. There was more. Underneath the triangle was another set of initials:

J.M.

Janet Macavity?

Jeremiah Mercer.

I stared at the paper for a few moments, then set it on my desk, next to the clutter that had accumulated over the past few days. I'd have to work on the puzzle later. The mess on my desk had set off a new bell. I had a newspaper to publish, and it was going to be another late night. Especially without Miah's help.

When my door burst open just after 9:00, I was working on an article profiling the African frogs that were invading the Jumping Frog Jubilee. Mayor Ellington stood in the doorway, trying to look angry wearing a frog hat and frog-logo T-shirt. It just didn't work. I had to stifle a laugh.

"Goddammit, Westphal, if you're planning to print anything about what happened...well, you can't! It'll ruin the Jubilee!"

I sat back in my chair and crossed my hands over my abdomen. I felt like a high-powered newspaper executive.

"Print what, Mayor?"

"Anything! Anything about this situation that's come up."

I thought he might leap, what with that frog shirt on, but he only bounded into the room, slamming the door behind him. Lot of slamming going on around here, I thought. Good thing I can't hear. I bet it was loud.

"This 'situation,' Mayor, is called murder. And it's news. People have a right to know about it. After all, they may be in jeopardy, too."

"You're just trying to sell your little newspaper, based on slanderous hearsay and libelous gossip! You know how much we need the income from this event, Westphal. If people find out someone was...killed...it will send them away in droves."

Say it, don't spray it, I thought, as I wiped his spittle from my cheek.

"Mayor, you can't stop the press from reporting the news. And this may go national. After all, everyone's heard of the Jumping Frog Jubilee. My little paper is a drop in the media bucket. So why don't you spend your time trying to find out who really killed Dakota and why, instead of threatening me and my newspaper."

"You don't know the meaning of the word 'threatening,' Westphal. If you print anything about Dakota's death, you won't have a newspaper anymore, I guarantee that. I'll sue you for everything you've got, expose you for what you really are, and turn your rag into nothing more than a birdcage liner, you hear me?"

I tapped my ear.

"You know what I mean, goddammit!"

Odd. The mayor seemed unusually upset, even for a reactionary like him. Did he really feel that strongly about the Jubilee being in jeopardy? Or was there something else behind his anger?

I stood up. "Listen, Mayor. I won't print anything that isn't true, you know that. But this could help Miah. Simonie Scott is accusing him of murdering Dakota Webster, and if my newspaper can help find the real killer, I'm going to do everything I can to find out the truth—"

"And your little contest is off the schedule."

"You can't do that. You're not the committee. You can't make those kinds of decisions."

"We'll see about that. I virtually run that committee. I didn't become mayor just 'cause I'm good at kissing babies, you know."

The thought of Mayor Ellington kissing a baby made me want to puke. I'd never let him kiss my frog, let alone my baby. But was he kissing up to someone on the committee?

"I'll see you tomorrow morning at the opening ceremonies, Mayor, with the winner's T-shirt for the worst verse." I moved to the door to show him out. When I opened it, Dan stood in the doorway poised to knock.

"What the hell's going on in here?" he said, lowering his raised fist.

Mayor Ellington, still standing by my desk, spun around and fled the room, flinging a few last words at me that I couldn't read.

Dan watched him go, then entered my office, closing the door behind him—gently.

"I gather he doesn't want you to print anything about the murder, eh?"

I nodded. "You're some detective."

"I heard him through the walls."

"Show off. Well, he's an idiot. How did he ever get elected?"

"The Clampers like him. That renegade group carries a lot of clout around here, as you know. So, anything new on the murder?" Dan sat on the corner of Miah's desk and glanced around at the piles of papers.

I remembered the graphic I'd discovered on Miah's computer and reached for the print-out on my desk. "Yeah, I found this on—"

The copy was gone. I rustled through the pile of papers once more, thinking I might have buried it under my notes. Nothing.

"Something missing?"

"The mayor! Damn him. He took the print-out of Miah's note."

I moved around to Miah's chair and ditched Woody Woodpecker again. The annoying bird was replaced by Miah's cryptic graphic. I hit "print," waited for the copy, and handed it over to Dan.

He studied it a moment. "What's this supposed to mean?"

"Not sure. Looks like Miah was thinking about Dakota. Maybe he was doing a little sleuthing of his own."

"Did he type this before or after Dakota was killed?" Dan asked.

That stopped me for a second. "Don't know. Probably before. It looks like some sort of triangle."

"Dakota, linked to Simonie and that other nurse, Holly Samuels. With his own initials at the bottom. Have you asked Miah about this?"

"Not yet. I will when I see him. What about you? Any news?"

Dan shrugged. "I was checking around the night shift at the hospital, trying to find out what kind of guy Dakota was. Seems he was a charmer. One woman called him a 'pimp.' That's slang for a playboy, I guess. Anyway, a lot of women knew him. He seemed to be well liked. Only one thing..."

"What?"

"I ran into Holly Samuels again. She didn't have such nice things to say. But she didn't go into any detail. Claimed she couldn't talk because she was on duty. Kept looking over her shoulder. Weird. Anyway, we have a date to chat tonight after she gets off work."

I actually felt a tinge of jealousy. "A date, huh. You're going to the hospital to talk to her?"

"No, she wants to meet me somewhere besides the hospital. She says the place is like a soap opera. We're meeting at He's Not Here in Angels Camp around eleven. Wanna come along?"

I relaxed a little and checked my watch. "I've got a ton of

work to do before then, but I hope to be finished. I sure could use Miah's help, though. Got to find someone to drop off the layout at the printer. Why don't I meet you there, in case I have to do it myself."

Dan hopped up from the desk. "Sounds good. I'm kind of glad you're coming. She makes me a little uncomfortable."

"In what way?"

"I don't know. Can't put my finger on it. But having you there will help. I just hope she doesn't clam up."

"If she does, I'll go flirt with some guy and let you handle it."

"Yeah, right." Dan grinned. "You want to go by the creek early in the morning, check things out again? I have a hunch we might have missed something."

"So now that you're an official P.I. you have hunches? Like what?"

"Don't know. Hunches don't tell you that much. They just make you do things when you can't explain why."

"I've got so many hunches, I don't know where to begin."

"I had a hunch you did."

I had a hunch he was about to kiss me. I was right.

I saw no sign of Miah the rest of the evening, so I had to do most of the last-minute work myself. It wasn't like him not to show up at all, but I'd had a feeling he was in no mood to do newspaper work. I couldn't blame him.

I was hoping the *Eureka!*, a weekly paper, would finally beat the five-days-a-week *Mother Lode Monitor* to a major story. But I couldn't shake the guilt that had edged up inside me. Was I helping or hindering Miah by writing the story? In other words, what were my true motives for getting the word out—selling newspapers like the mayor said, or helping my assistant clear his name?

I read the header once again: LOCAL JUBILEE CONTESTANT FOUND DEAD; KILLER SOUGHT. Next to it was a picture of Dakota taken from his high school yearbook. It was no *Enquirer* headline, but it would sell newspapers. And maybe, just maybe, it would help smoke out whoever killed Dakota Webster.

By 10:30 I was finished and ready to take the copy to the printer. As usual, they worked graveyard shift to have the paper ready for distribution by 4:00 in the morning. A small staff of handlers, mostly housewives trying to make a few extra dollars, would collect the bundles and tote them off to the various small towns of the Gold Country chain. By 6:00 A.M., every citizen would have access to the story.

By 6:05 I expected all hell would break loose. Especially in the mayor's office. I wondered how Miah would take the story. In the spirit it was written, I hoped. I hadn't mentioned his name.

I arrived at the He's Not Here saloon by 11:15 P.M. Only a few stragglers still hugged the long mahogany bar, hunched over shots of whiskey, bourbon, vodka, and the occasional microbrews. Pool tables filled the room, a jukebox glowed in a far corner, and the smell of alcohol was stronger than that of the bowls of peanuts on the bar. The place probably looked just about the way it did back in 1862 when it was built. All the saloon needed for authenticity were the swinging double doors, now replaced by solid oak.

Dan sat alone at the far end of the bar, presumably to see whoever came in. I waved, ignored the grins of three grizzled prospectors who hadn't seen razors since Gillette invented them, and sat next to Dan. He had a sweating Sierra Nevada waiting for me. No glass. Just the way I like it. He met my eyes and winked.

"She isn't here yet?" I asked, glancing toward the ladies' room.

"Nope." Dan took a long swallow of his beer.

"How long have you been here?"

"About half an hour. You're late."

"I know. It took a little longer than I thought. Are you sure she's coming?"

"I'm never sure of anything, especially when it comes to women. But she said she'd be here. So I assume she'll come. Unless..." He trailed off.

"Unless what?" I felt a chill down my spine, and it wasn't the beer.

"Unless she got hung up somewhere. Maybe at work. An emergency. Who knows?"

I said nothing, but we both knew that the way things were going, anything could have happened to delay her. Like Dakota had been "delayed"? We waited in silence, sipping our beers and watching David Letterman on the fuzzy TV set. The show wasn't captioned, and the TV was too far away to read lips clearly. I watched Dave put on a funny hat, grin at the camera, wave to his band, and tap his pencil until I grew bored. It didn't take long.

While Dan stared at Dave, I glanced at the man two stools down the bar. He looked much more interesting, with a beard down to his chest, arms as hairy as a monkey's, and a chain linked from his belt to his wallet. On the bar, in a small cage, was the fattest frog I'd ever seen.

I turned to face him. "You entering that in the Jubilee tomorrow?" I asked.

"Yep," he said, sticking his finger in the cage. "Got me a champeen here. One of them African frogs. Good to jump over twenty feet, guaranteed."

"Wow. But it looks a little...hefty. Won't that slow it down?"

"Nah. Got stronger legs than the locals. Look at this span." The man took the frog out of the cage and stretched its leg to show me the length. The span was wider than his hand.

"Got any money on it?" I asked. Gambling on the frog-jumping contest was almost a bigger event than the Jubilee itself.

" 'Course. You want in?"

"No, I'm not a gambler. Just a watcher."

"Well, I wouldn't bet on those locals, I can tell you that. They're not doing too well this year."

"Really? Why not?" I—honestly—batted my eyelashes.

"Something in the water is what I hear. Pollution or whatever. And that champeen from last year croaked." He laughed at his pun. I tried to laugh, too.

"Do you know what happened?" I batted some more.

"Just that one of his competitors was jealous, killed the frog, then killed the trainer. I think the guy's been arrested. Sheriff's kid."

I shook my head. What was the point of publishing a newspaper in the Mother Lode? News about murder spread faster than news about a gold strike. Even the out-of-towners knew everything—and more.

"But this guy here, he's gonna hop big-time. Five thousand dollars' worth, I'm betting! Whoo-ee. Sure you don't want a piece of the action?"

"Thanks, but I'll cheer you from the side. Good luck."

"Can I buy you a drink?" he said suddenly.

That drew Dan's attention away from Letterman—finally. He leaned around me, gave the guy a look, and the frogman slunk back. I smiled and turned my attention to Dan.

"Thanks a lot. That happens to be my Deep Throat. I was getting all kinds of information out of him. Not to mention trying to find out the competition against your Ribicop, or whatever you named your frog."

"Oh yeah?"

"Yeah. How am I supposed to investigate with you around?"

"You know where he got all that information he just told you?"

I looked at Dan. His eyes met mine.

"You blabbermouth!"

Dan stood up and paid the bar tab. "I was just stoking him, trying to see if he'd heard anything."

"You told him about Miah?"

"Nah, he already knew that part."

"Are you leaving?"

Dan looked at his watch. "Almost twelve. I don't wait longer than an hour for any woman. She's a no-show." Dan put his arms around me and gave me a hug.

"What's that about?" I asked, teasing.

"I don't know. That guy you were flirting with. Kinda made me jealous."

I smiled. "Wanna come over and discuss it?"

"I'm right behind you."

But as I headed toward my Chevy, I had a feeling I couldn't shake, even through the beer buzz.

Something must have happened to Holly Samuels.

Chapter 10

SINCE IT WAS LATE, and we'd had beer, and morning was practically right around the corner, Dan slept over. At least, those were the excuses he gave to get into my bed. But I had trouble focusing on foreplay, with all that was hopping around in my head. Dan sensed my mood and didn't pressure me to continue.

In the morning, I showed him how grateful I was.

We showered together—to save water, of course. I dressed in my favorite jeans and a fresh, unripped frog T-shirt. This one read *Frogtown* and featured a giant amphibian leaping over a small rendering of Angels Camp. Dan put on his worn jeans and plain T-shirt but managed to make them look like the latest fashions for *Today's Manly Man*. The thin cotton shirt showcased the size and strength of his arms, and I took in a sharp breath when I saw him emerge from the back room.

"Mocha?" I managed to say, after dumping a bottle of Tylenol onto the counter. I took a pill with my mocha to temper the budding headache, left the remaining capsules there, and slipped the empty bottle into my backpack.

"Headache?" Dan took the hot drink from my hands.

"Stress," I said.

"Hangover." He took a sip of his mocha, slipped into one of the booths, and alternated between petting Casper, my signal dog, and drinking his mocha. After inheriting the fifties diner from my Cornish grandparents, I'd turned the back area into living quarters and renovated the kitchen to its original kitschy splendor.

"Cute shirt," Dan said, after looking over the frog design.

"Thanks. Yours is...too," was all I could say.

"You don't think it makes me look fat?" He flexed like a *Baywatch* lifeguard.

So we didn't get out the door as early as we planned. The crime scene could wait another thirty minutes.

After we'd had enough sex to last us the next hour or so, we headed for Critter's Creek. It was still early—just after 7:00 A.M.—and the fairgrounds wouldn't be open until 10:00. We had plenty of time to snoop around and still make it for the opening ceremonies. And the Worst Verse award.

"Did you know you put your shirt on inside out?" Dan asked, when we arrived at the creek bed.

I looked down. Sure enough, a pale frog was leaping the opposite direction over a faded town. "This is your fault. I dressed right once this morning. If it weren't for you and those arms of steel..."

Dan laughed. "Don't worry, I'll help you get dressed every morning, and make sure you don't go out looking like that again."

"Very funny. Could we get to work here? Before someone catches us returning to the scene of the crime and accuses us of the murder?"

We split up; he headed upstream and I went down along the creek bed. We didn't know what we were looking for, but I'm a firm believer in crime-scene language. There's always something else to find besides the victim—if you look with your brain along with your eyes.

I had wandered farther downstream than I had planned when I found what I was looking for among the manzanita, moss, and big oaks. A strong smell of decay wafted up from the creek.

More dead frogs lay sprinkled along the edge of the creek bed.

Hundreds of them had washed ashore at the narrowed section of the creek where the trees and underbrush grew most plentifully. I knelt and examined one of the frogs, using a stick to turn it carefully, but I could see no immediate cause of death. What was I expecting? Gunshot wounds? These frogs were actually healthy-looking—aside from the fact that they were dead. Just like the ones I'd seen yesterday, farther up the creek.

I pulled out the empty Tylenol bottle I'd brought with me and dipped it in the water for a sample. After securing the childproof top and wiping off the excess creek water from my hands on my jeans, I returned the bottle to my backpack.

As I stood up, I saw Dan heading down on the other side of the creek. He waved, and I gestured for him to join me.

"Find anything?"

I pointed to the collection of dry-docked frogs. He knelt down, poked them, then picked one up, examining it closely.

I knelt next to him. "I found some yesterday, too. All dead. What do you think happened to them?"

He shrugged. "Some kind of environmental poison, maybe?"

"Like…contaminated water?" I shivered. This might be bigger than I had originally imagined.

Dan glanced up and down the creek, then pointed to some circular brownish-green clumps. More frogs. More floaters.

"I don't know. There aren't any chemical plants around here that I know of. The closest businesses besides the fairgrounds are those self-storage buildings…and the hospital."

"That could be it. Or maybe some kind of chemical company comes out here at night and dumps their toxins into the water?" I asked.

"Maybe. But that would be an awful lot of trouble, not to mention a big risk. Why not just haul it over to a legal site if you're going to transfer it?" Dan thought for a moment, then added, "I suppose the hospital could inadvertently be dumping something toxic nearby. Or..."

"Or what?"

"It's also possible someone is polluting the water deliberately."

I stood up, feeling a little short of breath. "You think someone could be poisoning the creek on purpose? If the water really is tainted, you know what that could mean?"

Dan stood, frowning. "If it ties into a municipal water supply... Where does this creek begin?"

"I think it's a tributary of either the Stanislaus or the Tuolumne River. Part of it empties into Lake Don Pedro and part of it goes to Miwok Lake. Which, of course, veers off to..." I felt my heart skip a beat "...Miwok Reservoir."

Dan frowned. "Which means, if the creek is contaminated, depending on where the toxins have been dumped, the reservoir could be tainted as well."

"And our drinking water..." I couldn't finish the sentence. I had read stories about companies poisoning community water supplies by dumping their waste products, but never on purpose. And not in my backyard.

"It would explain why all the frogs in Critter's Creek are dead." Dan reached into his pocket and withdrew a small medicine bottle. "Here, you dropped this. I assume you brought it to take a sample of the water."

"Oh, it must have fallen out of my..." That was odd. I had just put the bottle in my backpack. I reached into my pack, rummaged until I felt the bottle, and pulled it out. "No I didn't! See?" I looked at the small container in Dan's hand.

"This isn't the one you brought with you?" He held it up to read the label. The white sticker was blank, except for the printed words: MOTHER LODE MEMORIAL HOSPITAL.

"Where did you find that?"

Dan indicated a bush not far from the one where Miah had been hiding. We headed over. Dan dug around for a few minutes while I searched the bushes nearby. We found nothing more.

"Well, we know where it came from originally—Mother Lode Hospital. But how did it get out here by the creek?" Dan held the bottle up once again. "It looks like it hasn't been here very long."

"What do you suppose was in it?" I took the container from him, opened the top, and sniffed inside. A strong medicinal smell I couldn't identify. "Maybe it was some kind of frog poison?" I said, half kidding.

We doubled back to the fairgrounds at a quick pace. "We've got to alert Sheriff Mercer about the dead frogs," I said. "But let's not tell Mayor Ellington for a while. He only needs one more reason to keep me from participating in the Jubilee, and I don't want to give it to him."

"But if the water is polluted, Connor, the people here could be affected."

I nodded. I couldn't argue with that.

Dan headed for the sheriff's booth while I went toward the stage, hoping to catch Del Rey and her sister and tell them the news before things got crazy. It was already 9:30, and we had promised to meet for coffee before the rescheduled opening ceremonies at 10:00.

The crowds were seeping in as the concession booths began to open. I watched several women with foil-covered dishes and wrapped bowls head for the Jubilee Cook-Off tent while a country-western band began setting up next to the stage. And the Jubilee wasn't complete without its Monster Truck Show, Demolition Derby, Bull Riders Competition, and Sheep Judging Contest.

Glancing around at the crowd that seemed to double in size every few minutes, I knew there'd be no stopping the Jubilee now. It was too late.

I felt the presence of someone behind my back. That and some spittle. I turned around to face a blazing Mayor Ellington, shouting at me. I caught him mid-sentence:

"...told you to stop interfering! Now look what you've done! You're going to pay for this, Westphal, if it's the last thing..." He shut his mouth, unable to go on, spun around, and stomped off toward the sheriff's tent. He reminded me of a giant frog with his bounding steps. I should have entered him in the jumping contest. I wondered what was upsetting him now. Or was it the same old thing?

When fifteen minutes passed and the sisters hadn't shown, I still wasn't worried. Del Rey had a habit of being late for everything but a funeral. But when I saw Dan running toward me from the sheriff's tent, I suddenly grew alarmed. He never ran.

He was panting when he reached me.

"What is it? Are they going to close down the Jubilee? Has someone been poisoned? Did you tell the sheriff about the tainted water?" Questions tumbled out like spilled popcorn.

"No—"

"Miah? Is he all right?"

"Yes, he's—"

"What, then? What's happened? I can see it in your face."

Dan held me gently by the shoulders. "Del Rey called the sheriff's booth, trying to get a message to you."

"What's wrong? Did something happen to Del Rey? Is she—"

"Will you let me talk?"

I took a breath and tried to calm myself, then nodded.

"Del Rey's at the hospital—"

"I knew it! She's been poisoned, hasn't she? Or worse!"

"Del Rey is at the hospital because her sister was just admitted. It seems she's had a bad reaction to a dose of insulin. That's all I know. Del Rey asked if you might—"

"Oh my God. Call her back. Tell her I'm on my way. And if you get a chance, tell the mayor to take the contest trophy and shove it up his—"

"Connor!"

I arrived at the Mother Lode Memorial Hospital in less than ten minutes. Nestled in the valley between Angels Camp and Flat Skunk, the newly rebuilt institution looked more like a plush health spa than an emergency medical center.

The hacienda-style buildings were surrounded by pine trees, lava rocks, and more manzanita. Four wings linked to form a large square that looked invincible from the outside, like a historic Spanish fort. Vines with purple flowers crept up the pale pink exterior walls, inching toward the tile roofs.

A plaza had been constructed in the center with wooden benches for recovering patients and waiting relatives. A large mission-style bell stood at the central entrance, as if to welcome the followers of Father Junípero Serra. Ornate cement fountains draped with colorful flowers flanked the large wooden doors.

I entered the wing at the left that said ADMISSIONS and stopped at the front desk, half expecting a robed missionary to greet me. All I got was a volunteer, a middle-aged woman named Natalie Rose, according to her crooked nameplate. Her plump arms were laden with magazines.

"Hi, may I help you?" she said.

"I'm looking for a patient. Del Ores Montez. Can you direct me to her, please?"

She set down the magazines, punched a key on a computer, and typed in the name.

"She's in Intensive Care in the Mission Dolores wing, down the hall past the cappuccino cart and to the right."

Mission Dolores. How ironic. The name meant "sorrows." Del Rey had told me her name meant "of the king." I wondered what Del Ores meant. "Of the gold"?

I hurried down the hallway, made the turn, and located a nurses' station just outside the Intensive Care Unit.

I waited a few seconds for the charge nurse to turn around and greet me. When she did, I almost couldn't speak.

"You're...Holly Samuels!" I sputtered. I double-checked her nameplate to confirm my outburst.

"You're ...that newspaper lady. Can I help you?"

"Yes, I've been wanting to talk to you, but right now I'm looking for Del Rey, I mean Del Ores Montez. I understand she's here. May I see her?"

Holly Samuels eyed me for a moment, then glanced down at a chart lying on the counter. "I'm afraid not. She's in Intensive Care. You'll have to wait outside in the waiting room."

"Could you at least tell me how she is?"

"I'm sorry, we can't give out that information unless you're a relative."

I'll bet she loved saying that.

"Well, could you check to see if her sister is with her and let her know I'm here?"

"I'm sorry. This isn't a message service, and I'm very busy. You'll have to wait—"

I caught a glimpse of a wave in my peripheral vision and turned.

"Del Rey!"

"Oh, Connor, I'm so glad you came!"

"Ladies," Holly Samuels interrupted, "you have to be quiet. This is a hospital. If you want to talk, you'll have to go into the waiting room. Please."

Del Rey nodded. I didn't want to make trouble, but I sure didn't like Holly Samuels's attitude. I deferred to my friend and followed her to the adjacent waiting room. Two young children were coloring magazines with felt-tip pens, and an old man slept in an uncomfortable-looking chair. Del Rey and I sat down on a tan fake-leather couch.

"Del Rey! What happened? Is she going to be all right?"

Del Rey began to tear up. I hadn't noticed earlier, but the skin under her red-rimmed eyes was smudged and puffy. She'd already been crying and was starting up again.

"I don't know, Connor. She went to the GetWell Clinic for a checkup and her medication. She came home, took her shot, and then collapsed. I called 911, and they rushed her here."

"How's she doing?"

"Not good. Her blood sugar is way out of control."

"What does that mean?"

"I don't know if I told you, but Del Ores became blind as a child when she contracted retinal neuropathy as a result of the diabetes."

"But diabetes is something the doctors can control today, right?"

"Usually they can, but something went wrong. They're not sure what yet, but she may have underdosed."

"Underdosed? On insulin? Was she...?" I couldn't finish the sentence.

"Suicidal? I don't think so. In fact, she was so excited about winning the contest. She couldn't wait to get up there on the stage and collect her award."

"Then how could this happen?"

"That's a good question."

"Will she be all right?"

Del Rey began to weep again. "I don't know. The doctors said she's in a diabetic coma. She could...die."

As I held Del Rey's hand, the Jubilee, the death of Dakota Webster, and the floating frogs in Critter's Creek seemed very far away.

Chapter 11

WE SAT QUIETLY for a few minutes, each lost in her own thoughts. Only a short time ago Del Ores would have received her trophy for the Worst Verse contest. Now she lay in a diabetic coma, unaware of her surroundings and her situation.

Abruptly Del Rey turned around. Coming toward us was the woman who had been with Simonie Scott last night. I couldn't remember her name until she came closer, then I read her nameplate. Janet Macavity.

"Yes?" Del Rey stood up to greet the woman.

"I'm Janet Macavity, director of the business office here at the hospital." She reached out a hand, and Del Rey shook it. She completely ignored me.

"What's wrong?" Del Rey said instinctively. Like me, she must have read the concern on Janet's face.

The woman forced a smile, took a deep breath as if she had the weight of the world on her shoulders, and proceeded. "There's a slight problem."

"Has something happened to my sister? Is she all right—"

Janet raised a hand to calm Del Rey. "I'm sure everything's going to be fine. The doctors here are—"

"Then what is it? What's wrong?" Del Rey insisted.

Janet frowned. "I'm afraid there's a situation with her Medicare program forms."

I was well aware of the Medicare forms and the Americans With Disabilities Act documents that often accompanied them. Sometimes the worst part about being disabled is the paperwork.

"I...I don't know anything about that...." Del Rey stammered. She looked at me for a clue.

I stepped forward. "I'm Connor Westphal, Del Rey's friend. We met earlier—"

She cut me off. "Yes, I remember. You're that newspaper reporter."

Her words were benign, but her facial expression made them seem like expletives. She returned her attention to Del Rey.

"Anyway, as I was saying, I need you to come by the office and take a look at her file. We have to process this as quickly as possible, or we may have to move her to another... facility."

Facility. A euphemism for a rest home or another less complete institution.

"What do you mean, another facility?" Del Rey's mounting concern showed in her face.

"Well, let's talk about that later after we've had a chance to go over the file. Will you come with me?"

Del Rey glanced frantically at me. I nodded, assuring her I was right behind her. The red tape of bureaucratic funding was certainly nothing new to me. I'd do what I could to help her wade through the jungle of government and medical documents.

We followed Janet Macavity through a maze of corridors, passing several areas under construction. Mother Lode Hospital was undergoing renovation, thanks in part to the money raised last year at the Jumping Frog Jubilee. But in order to compete with the two other hospitals in the Gold Country, MLH had, in my opinion, gone overboard.

Not that I minded the Cappuccino Café carts placed strategically around the various waiting rooms. But did the hospital really need an Exercise Spa? A Kiddie Korral? An Aesthetics Salon?

A Naughty Nightie Boutique?

And what had happened to the ubiquitous green walls, the smell of disinfectant, the lime green Jell-O and instant mashed potatoes? Now the walls sported colorful murals of old forty-niner life. You'd think the place was a museum instead of a hospital. The medicinal smell had been replaced by various potpourri scents. And patients could even order specialty gourmet foods, such as Key Lime Pie and Garlic Potatoes, from the Cafeteria Caterer.

Janet's office was tucked in a corner at the end of one wing. By the time we reached it, I was certain I'd need a map, a compass, and a guide dog to find my way back.

She opened the door and gestured for us to enter. Del Rey took the chair closest to Janet's desk, and I sat in the one nearer the door. Janet moved around her desk and sat down gracefully in her leather chair.

"It looks like..." Janet paused as she opened Del Ores's file and pulled out a handful of papers "...she was covered until about a month ago. And then apparently she used up the funding in her account. According to my calculations, she's no longer covered by Medi-Cal or Medicare."

"What?" Del Rey said, taking the papers from Janet's hand. I'm sure they were Greek to her, but Del Rey is an intelligent businesswoman. She'd figure them out, given time.

Unfortunately, we didn't have time. I reached over and took a handful from Del Rey. We both read over our collection of forms while Janet took a phone call. Del Rey glanced at me several times, frowning, but I kept examining the reports and forms. As well as I knew these government documents, the results came up Greek to me as well.

"This doesn't make sense," I said to Janet, after she hung up the phone.

"It is odd, I agree. But clearly she has abused her allotment and is no longer entitled to the free funds."

I didn't like the way she'd added the word "free." Granted, many people had biases against those who received stipends, but a hospital business administrator should have understood the need more than anyone.

"Could I take these home? I'd like to study them a little more."

"I'm afraid not. They belong to the hospital and can only be released to the patient."

"Or a close relative," said Del Rey firmly.

Janet nodded, grudgingly. "All right, I'll have to make copies. You can't take the originals, of course."

"Of course not," Del Rey said.

"If you'll wait here..." Janet Macavity collected the forms from both of us, stuffed them haphazardly in the file folder, and stepped out of the room.

"What a bitch," Del Rey said, not one to hold back her opinion. "What's her problem? It's like she takes this thing personally."

I nodded. "Something's wrong, but we'll get it worked out. I just need time to really go over the paperwork."

"We'd better do it fast before they kick her out of the hospital and put her in one of those depressing 'long-term care facilities.' They're nothing but custodial institutions." Del Rey shuddered.

I stood up and moved to the open door, anxious for Janet's return. Just as I peered down the hall, I noticed a nurse standing only a few feet away. She looked startled to see me. She stared at me for another moment, then quickly disappeared around the corner.

"Wait here!" I said to Del Rey, then I dashed out of the room toward the vanishing nurse.

I caught up with her just as she passed the Kiddie Korral. "Holly?" I called out.

The nurse froze in her steps. Slowly she turned to face me. Her red face matched the sunset on the mural behind her.

"You were listening in just then, weren't you?"

"What?" She scrunched up her face to match the question.

"At Janet Macavity's door. You were spying on us."

"That's ridiculous! I was just passing by. I didn't even know you were in there. Besides, why would I want to listen in on your conversation. I've got patients to take care of—"

"The lady doth protest too much," I said, crossing my arms.

"Excuse me?"

Shakespeare wasn't her forte. Maybe Sherlock was more like it.

"You're lying. You were eavesdropping. Why?"

I could see Holly bite the inside of her mouth. She glanced up and down the halls, then stepped backwards into the nearby pediatric waiting room, empty except for a young man asleep in a far chair.

I followed her in, and we both sat down on one of the new leatherette couches. Someone had drawn suns and flowers on this one, with permanent felt-tip pen.

"What's going on, Holly? Why are you acting this way? You've been holding onto something. And Dakota is dead and Del Ores is in trouble. If you know anything that can help us, please—"

She shushed me. I was probably talking too loud, even though I'd been trying to monitor my voice to keep it low.

With another glance around to see if anyone was listening, she began. "Look, I'm not one of the most popular nurses at MLH. In fact, I think I'm close to losing my job. And I can't afford that. But I can't stand what's going on around here either."

"What's that?"

"I work with these people, and I would hate for anything to happen to them."

"The other nurses?"

She shook her head vehemently. "No, the patients. Mostly the elderly and disabled."

"Go on."

"Look, if I tell you anything, you have to promise to keep me out of it. I know you have a newspaper, and I can't let this stuff out if I'm going to be named. You understand."

When it came to the newspaper business, having an unidentified source was practically like having no source at all. I hated it, but I understood. I nodded reluctantly.

"I think..." She glanced around nervously.

"What?"

"I think there's something going on with my patients."

"Like what? Do you suspect they're being..." My stomach tightened. I hated to say it aloud. "...euthanized?"

"Oh no. Nothing like that. At least, I don't think so. I think...they're being robbed."

"You mean, someone's coming in and stealing their stuff?"

"No, not that either. Stealing their money—their funding."

"Oh, you mean like being bilked in some way."

She shrugged. "Anyway, I think someone is using these old and disabled patients' accounts to get money from the government. Lots of money. Like, thousands of dollars."

"How do you know?"

"I...overheard someone talking."

You seem to have a knack for that, I wanted to say. I let her continue, uninterrupted.

"I can't say who. And I don't have any proof. But maybe, since you're a reporter, you could find out somehow, without me getting involved. I could try to help you get into the files, maybe."

"You have no proof of any of this?"

Holly Samuels shook her head.

"You just overheard it?"

She nodded.

"And you won't tell me who said all this?"

She looked pained. "I can't...."

I stood up. "Well then, I really have nothing to go on, no proof, no idea where to look or even what I'm looking for. In fact, I don't even see a motive for this kind of crime."

She pulled me back down to the couch.

"Look, I said I'd help you. I just can't...get involved, you know?"

I was getting tired of the routine. After all, I wasn't in the Witness Protection business. "No, I don't know."

"I told you! My job. I'm a single mother. I have to have this job to support my kid. I'm willing to help you as much as I can, but I can't afford to get fired."

"What's in it for you, Holly? What's your interest in this?"

"Well, first of all, I happen to care for my patients."

"But that's not everything, is it?"

She suddenly jerked up. I turned to see what she was staring at.

"Simonie!" I stood up.

She ignored me and faced Holly, lashing out at her. "You stupid bitch. This is all your fault. You tried to run Dakota's life, and when you couldn't, you tried to ruin it, didn't you? You're nothing but a jealous bitch." Simonie turned to me. "Don't let her con you, lady. She's one of the best liars on the planet. I'll bet she's pouring her innocent little heart out for you, isn't she? Poor single mother with a baby to feed, wah, wah, wah. Well, don't believe a word of it. Dakota didn't."

Simonie whirled around and stomped down the hall. I wondered if everyone on the first floor of the hospital could hear her angry steps. Everyone but me, of course.

"What was that about?" I looked at Holly. She appeared as pale as her white uniform.

Holly stood up and met my eyes. "She hates me." Holly wasn't as easy to lip-read as Simonie. Mostly it was her lack of facial expression.

"Why?"

"Dakota and I..."

Uh-oh. "You two were...involved?"

Holly nodded.

"Wow! And Simonie took him away from you?"

"She never took him away from me. I didn't want anything more to do with him, after..."

"After what?"

"He...refused to take responsibility."

"For what?" I asked, and then it dawned on me. "You mean..."

She nodded. "Yes. My son. Dakota Webster is—was—his father."

Chapter 12

SOME OF THE PUZZLE pieces were beginning to fall into place. But at the same time, I felt like I had pieces that would never fit the picture. It was as if two puzzles were mixed together, and I couldn't tell which pieces were which.

"Where have you been?" Del Rey asked when I returned to Janet Macavity's office.

"Making a hospital call," I said vaguely, glancing first at Janet, then focusing on Del Rey.

"Funny," Del Rey said. "Well, now that you're back, you want the latest?" Del Rey held out the file folder.

I took the file and opened it. Photocopies of the originals were stacked neatly inside: pages and pages of forms for Del Ores Montez. The last page was the cancellation form. It had been marked: "Funds depleted," circled in red. I looked for the total amount.

Del Ores had spent over one hundred thousand dollars in the last year.

I looked blankly at Del Rey. "What does this mean?"

Del Rey turned to Janet. "Want to explain it to her the way you explained it to me?" she said tightly.

"As I told Ms. Montez, it appears Del Ores spent her entire balance of government funds in a very short time. Therefore, she no longer qualifies for further financial assistance."

"Tell Connor how Del Ores supposedly used the money," Del Rey said.

Janet paused, as if collecting her thoughts. "It seems she ordered quite a lot of pharmaceutical products."

"Insulin, I assume," I said.

"And…" Del Rey kept her attention on Janet.

"And," Janet continued, "she's spent some time in a short-term care facility."

"Yes, and…" Del Rey repeated.

Janet shot Del Rey a sharp glance, then softened. "And she purchased several pieces of expensive medical equipment."

I turned to Del Rey. "Wait a minute. You're saying that Del Ores spent a hundred thousand dollars on drugs, care, and gizmos, and it's all gone?"

Janet Macavity folded her hands. "I'm afraid so."

"Do you want to tell Connor about the equipment Del Ores supposedly bought, or should I?" Del Rey continued.

Janet took a deep breath. "It appears she spent quite a lot of her financial aid on therapeutic equipment, things like a special bed, an IV setup, a wheelchair, but…" She glanced at Del Rey.

Del Rey crossed her arms, signaling Janet to continue.

"Well, I don't know that much about diabetes, but I don't think diabetics need a lot of equipment or therapeutic support unless they have kidney damage or something like that, which Del Ores didn't. Basically, they need insulin to control their blood sugar levels."

"So you're saying Del Ores spent all her assistance money on stuff she didn't need?"

Del Rey and Janet looked at me and said nothing.

"But why?"

"That," Janet said, "is a very good question."

Del Rey leaped from her chair. I had seen her anger building, but thought she'd be able to maintain. Apparently I was wrong.

"If you're insinuating that my sister somehow misused that money, you're sorely mistaken! Del Ores would never do anything like that." I could tell Del Rey was screaming. Her face was contorted, and tiny drops of saliva sprayed from her mouth.

"Del Rey—" I reached over to calm her, but she shook me off.

"I'm going to get to the bottom of this, Ms. Macavity, and find out why those hospital records are wrong!"

With that, she left Janet Macavity's office, slamming the door behind her.

"She's upset," Janet said weakly.

"Damn right," I said. "And with good reason, wouldn't you say?"

Janet shrugged. "It's happened before."

"What's happened before?"

She met my eyes. "Patient fraud."

"What do you mean?"

"I mean, some of the people who are entitled to subsidy, either from the government or from private HMOs, figure out a way to get the money instead of the services or equipment. Last year we had a case where an elderly man ordered a hospital bed, an oxygen tank, and a portable kidney dialysis machine—all paid for by Medicare. He wasn't even sick, just old. He turned around and sold the items and kept the money."

"He sold them? How? Who would buy things like that?"

"You'd be surprised. There are lots of people who need medical equipment and can't afford it, but aren't poor enough to get Medicaid. There's quite a black market for some items. Then again, sometimes it's just for drugs."

"And you really think Del Ores bought these things, then sold them on the black market for cash?"

"I have no idea. I'm just saying—"

"You're just saying a little too much, Ms. Macavity. I'd be very careful about that if I were you. Ever heard of slander?"

"I'm just saying, it's a possibility. Although we're very careful here at the hospital, it's happened in the past."

"Well, like Del Rey said, we'll find out what's behind this.

In the meantime, don't even think about releasing Del Ores to some kind of halfway health care place. She's staying here."

"Are you willing to foot the bill?"

I paused. "Yes." Then I got to slam the door on my way out.

When I reached my car, I was so angry I almost didn't notice the large manila envelope lying on the passenger seat. Someone had slipped it in through the crack I'd left in the window of my classic '57 Chevy. I glanced around the parking lot to see if I could spot anyone suspicious lurking nearby, but saw only a bunch of cars.

As I was about to pick up the envelope, my car began to rock.

Earthquake?

I turned to see if the other cars were bouncing, too, or if the hospital building was about to come tumbling down.

The earthquake stopped.

And grinned.

"Dan!" I rolled down my window. I could lip-read him easily through the glass, but as a "hearie," he needed the added assistance of a voice. "You nearly gave me a heart attack! What's with the earthquake impersonation?"

Dan bent down, resting his forearms on my windowsill. "Just getting even for that Shake-Awake bed alarm you have. Scares me every morning when it goes off. I saw you headed out here. Tried to call you, but you ignored me, as usual. It was the only way to get your attention, short of throwing something at you. And you hate that."

"I hate earthquakes, too. Even good-looking ones with arms the size of anvils. But enough about that. What did you find out?"

"Not much yet, but I'm going back to the office to play around on the Internet."

"Can you get information on Medicare?"

"Okay, and how about ADA?"

"You know about ADA?"

"Sure. As cops we had to know everyone's rights."

I smiled. "What will the Internet tell you?"

"For a start, it'll tell me how the whole government medical thing operates. And if my hunch is right, there are probably some loopholes in the program."

"Great. That's all we need—for disabled people to lose their hard-won rights to financial and medical aid, thanks to a bunch of scam artists."

"What's that?" Dan nodded toward the envelope lying on the car seat.

"Don't know. I found it there when I got to the car. Come in, and I'll let you have a look. If it's what I think it is, we may have some insider information on Mother Lode Memorial's patient funding."

I unlocked the passenger door as Dan came around the car and slipped into the seat. By then I had the contents of the envelope in my hand. One by one I looked over the photocopied sheets, handing each off to Dan as I finished.

"What do you make of this?" I held up the last sheet of paper. It was marked MEDI-CAL/MEDICARE at the top, just like all the others. The name underneath read "Joseph Swec." Each sheet contained a different name, some male, some female. The ages varied from fifty-one to eighty-four years. Diagnoses included melanoma, cirrhosis, angina, hematoma, myocardial infarction, multiple sclerosis. And diabetes. There were twelve sheets in all.

"No clue," Dan said.

I flipped through the pile again. "Twelve different names. Several different conditions, some the same. Varying ages, mostly middle-aged to elderly."

"No private health insurance," Dan added.

I looked at him. "Curiouser and curiouser."

Dan nodded. "As Lewis Carroll would say, 'No shit.' "

I dropped Dan off at his office and headed for my own office next door, hoping to get a moment to study the contents of the envelope without distraction. No such luck. Mayor Elijah Ellington sat in Miah's chair reading the latest edition of the *Eureka!*

"How did you get in?" I threw my backpack on my desk so I could pose with my hands on my hips and look really tough.

He shrugged. The posture didn't seem to impress him. "The door was open."

I shook my head. "I never leave my door unlocked. Not since my office was broken into a while ago. How did you get in?"

He put the newspaper down and stood up. "I told you, the door was open. In fact, I thought you were here. Called your name a few times till I realized you couldn't..." He flushed and couldn't complete the sentence. "You know...anyway..."

I glanced around to see if anything had been tampered with. Everything was still a mess, just the way I like it. Except that Miah's desk looked unusually clean.

"Did you touch anything?" I studied him, waiting for the lying-politician giveaway—a raised eyebrow, a sideways glance, sweaty palms wiped on polyester pants.

"Just your newspaper. In fact, that's why I'm here."

"Why? To read over my shoulder as I type up my copy? Sorry, free country, free speech, free press..." I was stumped after three "frees."

"Well, there won't be any get-out-of-jail-free if you print anything that could ruin this event. I'll see to that."

"Mayor Ellington, if you're finished with the clichés, I have a newspaper to run." I still get a tingle when I say that. I turned my back to him and sat down at the computer. He'd either leave or sneak up behind me and garrote me. I wouldn't have put it past him. The thought actually made me shudder. I turned to make sure that he wasn't holding any kind of rope or nylon stocking, but he'd vanished.

And so had the print-out on my desk of Dakota Webster's death—along with my personal thoughts about his murder.

Luckily I had everything on disk, but I still didn't want the mayor reading my mind.

Stupid mayor.

Before I reloaded the story from the disk, I pulled open the manila envelope stored in my backpack and laid out all twelve sheets on the floor so I could study them in one swoop. Someone had left these for me to see, so they must be important. But what was the significance? And how was I supposed to figure it out?

I reviewed the forms once again. Joseph Swec was sixty-four years old, admitted for angina. He'd been given nitroglycerin, had stayed in the hospital a week, then transferred to a short-term care facility in Flat Skunk.

Ann Parker, eighty-four, hospitalized for pneumonia, had been administered penicillin and sent back to her nursing home after two weeks.

Charles Anderson, seventy-three, admitted for diabetes, was given insulin and sent to—

My heart skipped a beat. Where was that nitroglycerin when I needed it? I leapt from the room, skidded on the hardwood floor in front of Dan's office, and shoved my way in, panting.

"Dan! Come quick! You've got to see this!"

I didn't give him a chance to respond. Instead, I spun around, ran back to my own office door, and flopped back down on the floor. Dan entered a few seconds later, wide-eyed.

"What?"

I waved him over and gestured for him to sit next to me on the floor. He knelt down and glanced at the papers displayed in front of me.

"Look!" I pointed to the same section on each of the papers. Each one was filled in with the same—or similar—information.

Dan read them aloud. "BeWell Health and Home Care Center. GetWell Health Care Center. StayWell Health Care. LiveWell Health Center…"

Dan looked at me. "Yeah? They're all short-term health care facilities. So?"

"You don't think that's odd?"

"Why is that odd?"

"None of these patients went home after staying in the hospital. They all transferred to some kind of rest home setup. Some of them even came from there to the hospital."

"So?"

"So, you don't think that's unusual?"

"No, why?"

"Because...because...that's the only thing these patients seem to have in common, other than being sick."

"I still don't get the connection, Connor." Dan stood. I rose with him.

"I'm going to pay a visit to one of these health centers and see what they have to offer," I said. "That's the only link I've got at this point. Have you made any progress on the websites?"

Dan shook his head. "I have a feeling I've got to wade through a lot of crap before I get to anything meaty. I'll let you know." He headed back to his office, leaving me to my own pile of crap in the middle of the floor.

And one niggling suspicion that wouldn't go away.

Chapter 13

I SAT DOWN AT my computer and logged onto the Internet. Yahoo was helpful in providing me access to several sites that offered health care in the Gold Country. I clicked on the first one—GetWell Health Care—located in Flat Skunk. The website was professionally designed, inviting and user-friendly, with graphics of happy sick people enjoying the luxuries of health care under the guidance of Casting Call nurses.

"We provide short- or long-term twenty-four-hour care for your loved ones, in a warm atmosphere with a caring staff, the best medical provisions, and cheerful patient rooms." The ad went on, listing the perks of staying with GetWell, including on-site activities, personalized exercise, organic health food, and so forth. The only things missing were the waterfront views of the ocean and free valet parking.

I clicked down, and was about to head for another one of the health care sites on my list when I noticed links at the bottom of the page. Three more places were included. I clicked on the first one—LiveWell Health Center—and brought up their site. This one was located in Angels Camp. The web design was similar to the first one. I tried the next two. They also had similar designs, and were located in the Gold Country towns of Murphys and Bogus Thunder.

It was beginning to look like a chain of health care facilities, but with slight variations on the names.

None of the websites listed the owners. That would take

some digging. But I had a feeling the same person who owned the center in Flat Skunk also owned the others in the Mother Lode area.

And if memory served, that would mean our very own frog fanatic. Carrie Yates.

I knocked on the door of GetWell Health Care, located on the outskirts of Flat Skunk. The building was really just an old house, remodeled to create the atmosphere of a "hospital in a home."

Generic signs with the words QUIET and NO SOLICITORS were carved out of wood and découpaged. A white picket fence painted with cows outlined the trim lawn that sported empty deck chairs, also decorated with farm animals. A BMW sat next to an ambulance in the driveway off to one side, behind a tall pine that held a two-story birdhouse, complete with paintings of birds. As I stepped up to the front door, the sign, featuring little ducks, read WELCOME TO GETWELL!

Not a good place for diabetics, I thought, grimacing at all the sugarcoated cutesy stuff.

After several moments the door opened. Burnett Pike stood in the doorway looking confused, as if he were trying to place me.

"Hello, Mr. Pike. I'm Connor Westphal. From the *Eureka!* newspaper?"

His face tensed and his hands balled into fists. "I'm sorry, my wife's not giving interviews about LEAP right now. She's...not feeling well." He started to close the door.

I pressed against it with my hand. "Wait, Mr. Pike! I'm not here for the newspaper. I was just trying to introduce myself. I...I'm looking for care, for my uncle...Uncle Danny."

The door slowly opened again.

"Is your uncle ill?" he asked, still looking puzzled.

"Yes, uh, he has diabetes and...needs some specialized care. I wondered if I could ask you a few questions about your services. You came highly recommended to me."

"By who?"

By whom, I wanted to say. It was the writer in me. Instead I said, "By a patient you had years ago. I'm not sure you'd remember—Casper Smith." Casper Smith. The only two names I could come up with on short notice—my dog and my boyfriend. Jeez.

"I've only been here for a short time, but I'm sure Carrie would remember. Anyway, this isn't a good time. Like I said, my wife isn't feeling well—"

"I won't keep you then. I just wondered what you had to offer for my uncle."

He turned, reached behind him, then handed me a brochure. "We have a webpage—"

"I went there. It was very helpful. I just had a quick question. Do you still take in diabetics?"

"Of course. We're here to assist disabled, elderly, any short-term chronic care patients, especially those with strokes and heart problems."

"What happens if the patients should suddenly require urgent medical care? Say, if my uncle went into a diabetic coma or something?"

Burnett Pike raised an eyebrow. "A diabetic coma?"

I may have sent up a red flag. I'd have to be a little more discreet with my questions. "Yes, he's gone into two comas in the past couple of years. What do you do in situations like that?"

"We immediately transfer them to the local hospital, which would be Mother Lode Memorial, for emergency care and further treatment. Patients only stay with us as a sort of interim or halfway house, until they can go home."

"Great. Well, thanks for answering my questions. May I come back when your wife is feeling better to tour the place and see if it's what my aunt might want?"

"You mean your uncle?"

"Did I say aunt? Yes, I meant my uncle. As a matter of fact, my aunt will probably be needing care soon, too." I hoped it was a plausible recovery. He didn't seem to notice.

"Of course." With that, Burnett Pike closed the door.

I stood on the doorstep, brochure in hand, wondering what was up with Carrie Yates, the seemingly ever-suffering wife.

The Nugget Café was bustling when I entered a little after noon. All ten booths were occupied, and there wasn't a single stool available at the counter. I was about to consider getting something to go when I spotted the back of a familiar head of hair. Dark. Curly. Sexy, even from behind.

"Is this seat taken?" I asked, sliding into the booth opposite Dan. I caught him with a mouthful of his favorite, Mama Cody's meatloaf, heavy on the catsup.

"Gwumpf, gumble," he said. That's all I could make out with the obstruction of food in his mouth. I nodded like I understood him, then waved Jilda over to place my order. She gave me the hold-on-a-sec sign.

Dan swallowed, ran his tongue around the inside of his mouth, then took a deep pull on his Sierra Nevada Pale Ale. He doesn't drink the darker stuff until nightfall.

"What's up?" he finally said. "You look like the cat who swallowed the canary."

"Wrong. The cat who swallowed the canary looks that way 'cause he's guilty. I'm not guilty of anything."

"Yet."

I picked up the salt shaker and shot him a blast of crystals. "It just so happens I paid a visit to GetWell Center, the one owned by Carrie Yates and her husband, Burnett Pike."

Jilda swung by on her rounds of the restaurant. "Quit throwing the merchandise, willya, Connor? What do you want—your usual?"

I nodded and she headed for the next table.

"What were you doing there?"

"Finding respite care."

"For who?"

"For you. They're expecting you next week."

"Fine with me. I wouldn't mind being waited on hand-and-foot by a couple of cute nurses."

"Your nurse is Frank."

"Short for Francesca, I hope."

"Short for Franco 'the Needle' Capone. You'll love him."

Jilda brought my usual BLT with a side of potato salad and a Sierra Nevada. I signed, "Thank you" and she tried to sign, "You're welcome" but it came out, "I'm horny." The two signs look fairly similar if you're a sloppy signer. Or maybe she really meant she was horny. With Jilda, who wore her tops low-cut, her midriff bare, and her pants tight, anything was possible.

"So what did you find out?" Dan said, after he stopped watching Jilda move away from the table. I was tempted to throw the shaker this time, but I held back.

"Not much. Carrie was 'indisposed.' Burnett answered some of my questions about how the place is run, that kind of thing. But he wasn't in much of a mood to sell me a room with a view. Seemed preoccupied. Said he was concerned about his wife."

"He had good reason. The woman's a nutcase."

"Not all frog fanatics are nutcases, you know."

He took another pull on his beer. "And while you were out trying to commit me, I was doing some Internet checking."

"What did you find out?"

"I got sidetracked. Ended up checking on government regulations for private health care services. They aren't."

"They aren't what?"

"Regulated."

"You're kidding."

"Not by the U.S. government, at least. Only by local jurisdictions. The Gold Country area has some of the most lenient laws. All you have to do to set up shop is show that you're providing assistance to the disabled, elderly, or those with chronic diseases, and you're in business."

"You mean, there's no government oversight?"

"County health department checks to see that the place is clean, and there's no blatant abuse of the patients, but other than that, not much."

"Wow. What happens if the patients need more specialized medical care?" I asked.

"If it's urgent, they're transferred to the local hospital for treatment. Then they're returned to the health care center when they stabilize."

"I guess that's a good enough check-and-balance system. If abuse is going on at those places, the hospital would probably recognize it after admitting the patient. They're always on the lookout for things like that."

"Maybe. But I'm sure there are ways of disguising mistreatment. At any rate, that's not the issue here. The issue is, why did Del Ores lose all her benefits?"

I thought for a moment, nibbling on my BLT. Too much mayo, as usual. I squeezed the bread and let the excess drip down onto the plate, forming tiny white pools. "Dan, does the hospital benefit from health center assistance or does it lose money?"

"It benefits the hospital when a patient comes in under emergency or urgent-care status. That raises the hospital's census, which enables them to bill Medicare for reimbursement. More patients using more expensive services means more highly trained staff, more equipment, and more claims for reimbursement from the government assistance programs."

"In other words, more money."

Dan smiled. "You did the math."

"Is there any way to steal the government's money in cases like this?"

"I'm not sure. Haven't tried it myself lately."

"What if...somehow both the hospitals and the health care centers are getting money from the government—say, double-billing. Would that be possible?"

"I doubt it. That would be too easy to uncover. They'd both be caught within the first fiscal period."

I thought some more. "What if the patients are being used in some way to get more money?"

"How?"

"I don't know."

"There's only one way I can think of to bilk the program out of funds, and that's to send a patient home—"

I cut him off, "— and not report it."

Dan nodded.

I smiled.

"That way, the hospital—"

"—or health care center," Dan added.

"Or health care center, could continue submitting requests for reimbursement, yet not have to spend the money on any patients."

"But could that work?" Dan asked, bursting my fast-inflating balloon.

"Good question. And if so, who would be behind it? Would the hospital and health care center have to work together?"

"Not necessarily," Dan said. "But even so, how could you prove any of it?"

I swallowed the last bite of my sandwich. "Gotta run," I said, sliding out of the booth. I dropped a five-dollar bill on the Formica table.

"Where are you going?"

"Gotta check into the hospital."

"You sick or something?"

I didn't have time to explain my meaning. Better to let him think I might be sick. Maybe I'd get chocolate and flowers out of it.

Chapter 14

JANET MACAVITY looked up. "You again?" I thought she said.

"I beg your pardon?"

She went on, but this time I noticed she had her finger pressed on her intercom button. "I can't possibly make it by two-ten. See if you can back it up." She lifted her finger from the button and smiled at me.

I gave a small laugh. "Heh, I thought you were talking to me. I thought you said, 'you again,' but you were saying, 'two-ten.'" I realized the woman was looking at me as if I might be a mental patient from the 5150 ward. "Never mind. I wondered if I could ask you a couple more questions?"

Janet checked her watch. "If you make it fast. It's busy today. And I'm not sure I can answer your questions anyway. I've told you everything I can."

I stepped in and slipped tentatively into the chair opposite her. I'd have to phrase my questions carefully, or she might stop talking altogether.

"Since you're in charge of the business office and you know how things run at the hospital, can you tell me exactly how the money from Medi-Cal and Medicare is distributed? How is it accounted for?"

Janet folded her hands. It was one of those try-to-be-patient gestures I'd seen the school principal use when I got in trouble. Usually for not listening.

"It's handled very carefully, Ms. Westphal. That's the one thing I hate about this business—the forms. The paperwork is overwhelming. That's why so many doctors hate Medicare, Medi-Cal, and Medicaid. The government makes it so hard to cooperate."

I didn't need the injustice lecture. Just the facts, ma'am. "So it would be impossible to defraud Medicare and Medi-Cal?"

"Nooo, I wouldn't say that. With today's computer hackers, I'm sure there are ways to manipulate the funds. But it wouldn't be easy. And the risk would be tremendous. If you're caught, well, you go to prison." She looked down at the pile of papers on her desk.

"The hospital benefits from the services, though, doesn't it?"

She met my eyes again. "We receive funds, of course, to help care for the patients. But we hardly make a profit."

"But you do hire more staff, right? Order more equipment? And bill the government for these expenses?"

"Of course, if we have to."

"And that makes Mother Lode Memorial Hospital a better facility, am I right?"

"We hope so."

"Which attracts more patients in general, I suppose."

"I suppose."

"So everyone benefits—the patients, the hospital, the staff, even the health care centers who send their patients for urgent or emergency care."

"Yes."

"Everyone except the government. The taxpayers. The money's got to come from somewhere, right?"

"Yes, but I don't see—"

"Tell me about the hospital's relationship with health care centers. How does that work?"

Janet checked her watch again. "I really must—"

"Do you make money off of them?" I find that more direct

questions tend to keep the conversation on track—and make the defensive interviewees forget about their watches.

"No, of course not. It's a mutually beneficial arrangement. They care for patients who don't need the expensive day-to-day care we offer in the hospital, but we're here for them if more medical intervention is needed."

"Do they pay you?"

"No, of course not."

"And the hospital doesn't offer any subsidy to the centers?"

"No, why would they?"

I shook my head. I'd hoped Janet might open another door for questioning, but it appeared that I was at a dead end. I was sure there was something I should be asking her, but I didn't know what.

I shouldn't have paused. That left Janet a moment to check her watch again and remember her other obligations. She stood. I joined her and reached out to shake her hand. "Thanks for your time."

Janet limply shook my hand. Her fingers were tense and cold, her grip weak, and her palm slightly sweaty. It wasn't a pleasant sensation.

I was halfway to my car when someone tapped me on the shoulder. I was surprised to see Janet Macavity again, slightly out of breath. "You're a fast walker," she said, panting.

I waited for her to go on, wondering why she had chased me down. Had I forgotten something in her office?

"I thought of one more thing just after you left. It might help."

This was an unexpected turnaround for a woman who seemed so protective of her position and her hospital.

"Great! What is it?"

"When you mentioned the centers, I got to thinking."

Fast thinker. "What about them?"

"Well, there have been a couple of times when the center was supposed to send us a patient and the patient never arrived."

I blinked—and it wasn't because of the sun in my eyes. "What do you mean?"

"Are you familiar with the GetWell Health Care Center? The one owned by Monko Yates?"

"You mean Burnett Pike and Carrie Yates?"

"Yes, sorry. Monko was Carrie's first husband. He's the one I worked with until he died last year. That's just it. Ever since Carrie took over the business, things have been pretty sloppy there."

"You mean in terms of sanitary conditions?"

"Oh, no. It's clean enough. But the paperwork—it's not always done correctly. Or it takes forever to come back to us. I just thought you might want to know. According to her chart, Del Ores visited the place to get more of her insulin. Maybe there's a connection."

I nodded. "Thanks. You may be onto something."

"I've...been a little troubled by them lately. When Carrie married Burnett Pike, I got the feeling...never mind. I'm talking out of turn."

"Do you suspect something's going on there?"

"I'm just saying, if you want to get a fuller picture of how the funding works, I'd recommend you check them out. I'd known Monko for a long time. And Carrie, but not as well. Still, I don't think she'd ever do anything...dishonest. But that new guy she married... Things changed after he came along and... Listen, I've got to get back. Sorry I can't be more help. And I'm sorry about this thing with Del Ores Montez. We'll try to work something out."

Janet Macavity turned and headed back to Mother Lode Memorial, looking as if she had the entire hospital business office on her back. She probably did. But what really puzzled me was her sudden cooperative attitude. What was that about?

When I returned to GetWell, Burnett Pike didn't answer the

door. Instead a nurse wearing a uniform two sizes too small for her greeted me with a tired face.

"Visitin' hours are over," the nurse said in the way of greeting. "Come back tomorrow between eleven and one." She started to close the door. People were always doing that to me.

I held a hand up. "I'm not a visitor," I said. I dug through my backpack, found my notebook, and pulled it out, along with my stash of multipurpose business cards. "I'm Sierra Williams, from the Calaveras County Health Department."

The card, in fact, read CALAVERAS PUBLIC SERVICES, a nice generic term I'd made up to work my way in where I didn't usually belong. Sierra Williams was the union of my grandmother's and grandfather's first names.

She took the card, gave it a brief glance, and met my eyes. "Yeah?"

"Is Burnett Pike in?"

"Not right now."

I pretended to check my notebook. "How about Carrie Yates?"

"She's indisposed."

"Well, I had an appointment to come take a look around." I stood my ground, staring her down like a lion about to lunge for her prey. After a few seconds she backed up, allowing me to pass.

"Thank you. Are you sure Carrie Yates is not available? I'd really like to talk with her."

"She's in her room, sick. Can't go in there right now."

"Okay, well, I'll do a quick once-over of the place, just to please my boss, then get out of your way."

She eyed me suspiciously, then pointed out the different areas of the center. It was the supply room I was most interested in checking. As soon as she returned to whatever it was she did there, I reached for the door handle to the room that read NO ADMITTANCE. It even had one of those biohazard signs. That's always my favorite kind of place to enter.

The door was locked.

I called for Nurse Ratched, and she returned in a few moments, looking exasperated. "What?"

"This room is locked. Can you let me in?"

She nodded, whipped out the ring of keys she kept on her hip, and unlocked the door. Simple as that.

"Thanks," I said, expecting her to return to her work again.

She didn't. She stood by the door watching me as I entered the room. I moved slowly around the collection of strange-looking medical equipment and boxes of medical supplies until I noticed a glass-front medicine cabinet. I peered in, then tried the door. Locked.

I turned to the nurse, but she shook her head. "Can't go in there. Sorry. Besides, you should know that."

I nodded, hoping she didn't suddenly decide to call the county and check on me. Trying not to look nervous, I studied the cabinet door. It was glass with wire running crisscross through the panes. Inside I could read the names of some of the pharmaceuticals: insulin, vitamin K, penicillin, nitroglycerin. I turned to ask the nurse a question when she herself turned toward the front door, then disappeared from my view.

I had a feeling the jig was up.

She reappeared in a matter of seconds. "Sounds like Mr. Pike is back if you want to talk with him. That's his car pulling in now."

Uh-oh. I virtually skipped across the room and ducked outside, hoping the nurse would lock the door before Burnett Pike caught me snooping around his supply cabinet. That would be tough to explain.

Beads of sweat began to form along my forehead as I envisioned him getting out of the car, closing the door, and heading up the walkway. It wasn't that far from the driveway to the front door. I watched the nurse turn the key in the supply-room lock, just before the front door swung open.

"Mr. Pike!" I said, probably too loudly. "You're back!"

"She's from—" the nurse began, but I cut her off.

"Mr. Pike knows who I am. Thank you, Nurse. Mr. Pike, I have a few more questions for you. I wonder if we could talk, alone?"

The nurse frowned but said nothing more. Burnett nodded at her, and she slipped out of the room without another word. Thank God.

"You're the young woman who was here earlier. You said you have an uncle you want to admit—"

"Yes, you remembered! Great. It's become rather urgent, and I'd like to get him in as soon as possible. Could I ask you just a few more questions?"

"I suppose. Although, like I told you, my wife is sick. She may need my attention."

"I understand. Is she terribly ill?"

He shook his head. "Not too bad. Luckily we have everything she needs right here."

"It must be handy living in a health care center when you're sick."

"True. But it makes it harder on me when she's under the weather. I have to manage the whole place by myself. And I only got into the business a few months ago, after she starting having her spells."

"Is it anything serious?"

"No. The doctor's given her a prescription. She'll be all right. Just takes time."

He was being awfully evasive about his wife's illness. But then, it was none of my business. I asked Burnett a few bogus questions about my Uncle Danny's care, and he answered them. Then I segued into more general questions about the center itself.

"How does the financial aspect work?" I asked.

"If your uncle's entitled to Medicare, which I'm sure he is, then he'll qualify for all financial concerns."

"Great. Uh, how big a facility is this?"

"We've got eight rooms."

"And you have something available right now?"

"Oh yeah, we got plenty of room. We only have two patients right now."

Two patients. I wondered how the couple made enough
money to live on.

"You say you just recently took over the business?"

"Yeah, Carrie was a widow. Just lost her husband. He really ran the place after he quit working at the hospital. She
didn't want much to do with the business, so I took over when
we got married a few months later. I'm the one who got the
business out of the red—"

He stopped abruptly and turned toward a doorway that led
to another part of the center.

"I'm sorry. My wife. She's...calling." He suddenly looked
frantic. I wondered what he meant by *calling*. "If you'll excuse
me, I really have to go. Can you let yourself out?"

I nodded and thanked him, but I don't think he really heard
me or cared. He was out of the room before I could finish the
last word.

As I stepped toward the front door, I took one look back.
GetWell Health Care was a strange operation, but I couldn't
put my finger on what bothered me about the place. It seemed
to be perfectly fine—clean, staffed with registered nurses,
plenty of room, access to medical care.

But personally, I wouldn't want to be caught dead there.

Chapter 15

SHERIFF MERCER was fiddling with his new hearing aid when I entered his office. With his back to me, he didn't hear—or see—me come in. I thought about sneaking up behind him and scaring him, but I figured he might shoot me. Cops are like that. I decided to stamp my foot instead. The sheriff turned around, his hearing aid dangling from his right ear.

"Hey, Connor. Didn't see you come in." He wiggled his aid around, stuck his finger in his ear to secure the ear mold, and fluffed the fringe of his hair back down over his ear where he'd messed it up.

"How's the hearing aid?"

He shrugged. "Driving me nuts. It's either too loud or it's picking up too many sounds or it's squeaking or the batteries are dead. Pain in the ass, if you ask me."

"But you can hear better, right?"

"I suppose." He sat down at his desk and halfheartedly riffled the ever-present pile of papers in front of him.

"You'll get used to it. Besides, there are some gadgets out now that can personalize the aids to your specific needs. Have you been to the SHHH group meeting I told you about?" I'd recommended the hard-of-hearing support group when I'd first learned the sheriff was going deaf.

He shook his head. "Haven't had time. This case is driving me nuts, too."

With Del Rey's sister in the hospital in a diabetic coma, I'd almost forgotten about Dakota Webster's murder. And Jeremiah Mercer's questionable involvement.

"Anything new?" I sat down opposite him so I could read him better. Since he'd begun losing his hearing, he'd become more sensitive to my need to face him.

Sheriff Mercer frowned. His expressions are so clear and distinct that sometimes I can even read different frowns. But this time the grooves were deeper than usual. He held up what looked like some kind of report.

"Just got the water sample results back."

"Was the creek poisoned?"

"Not exactly."

My turn to frown. "What do you mean, not exactly?"

"Well, the water wasn't exactly pure creek water. But there wasn't anything especially toxic. Just traces..."

"Traces of what?"

"Drugs."

"You mean like...cocaine or heroin or something?"

"No, more like vitamin K and erythromycin and nitroglycerin. And insulin."

I was dumbfounded. "You're kidding! What...?"

"You got me. Only thing I can figure is, someone came along and dumped a bunch of pharmaceuticals in the creek for some reason, and I don't have a clue why."

"What about the ground water? Any concerns for the safety of the public?"

"They're still checking on that. It would take a lot to contaminate the drinking water and affect the community. But there was enough to document in the report. Now they're doing checks up and down the creek to find out the extent of it."

"Any chance the drugs could have killed all those frogs?"

"Sure. I wouldn't doubt they had something to do with the death of the frogs. Arthurlene is doing an autopsy."

"On Dakota? I thought she'd already done it."

"On a frog."

"Really!" I flashed on seventh-grade science class and the

frog I was assigned to pith and dissect. I couldn't do it. When
the teacher wasn't looking, I sneaked my frog out to the play-
ground and let it go, then made up the results using the book.
The teacher never caught on. I hoped Arthurlene hadn't done
the same in her science class. Apparently frog dissection did
have some merit.

"I should be hearing from her within the hour."

The phone light on Sheriff Mercer's desk lit up. While he
took the call, I sat slumped in my chair, pondering the latest
information. Medications had been dumped into the creek.
Why? To kill the frogs? What for? To reduce the competition?
Was the Jumping Frog Jubilee that important to Dakota?

To Miah?

Or to someone else?

The sheriff hung up his phone. That groove between his
eyebrows looked permanent.

I straightened up. "Who was that?"

Sheriff Mercer put his hand over his eyes and rubbed his
forehead. He mumbled something, but I couldn't read his lips
with his hand obscuring his face.

"What?" I said, leaning in to get his attention.

He lifted his head. "Ellington."

"What does our idiot mayor want now? A parade?"

"He's on his way over."

"Why?"

"He's bringing Peyton. Sheriff Locke."

My heart skipped a beat. I had a feeling I knew what that
meant.

Tears sprang to Sheriff Mercer's eyes. He rapidly blinked
them away.

"Sheriff, it's going to be all right. They don't have any evidence that can link Miah to anything. The mayor is just blow-
ing smoke, trying to protect his precious Jubilee. You'll—"

I never got a chance to finish my little "Up with Life"
speech. Mayor Ellington burst into the office, followed by
Sheriff Peyton Locke. She looked flushed as she entered, and

muttered something to Sheriff Mercer I couldn't read. But I had a feeling this was going to put a strain on their romance.

"Elvis—" Sheriff Locke began. She held a folded piece of paper in her hand.

"Sheriff!" Mayor Ellington snatched the paper and thrust it at Sheriff Mercer.

The sheriff took it but didn't open it. He glanced at Sheriff Locke.

"Mayor!" She glared at the mayor, then turned back to Sheriff Mercer, looking extremely uncomfortable. Their relationship had been developing nicely—until now. I felt for them both.

"That's a warrant for the arrest of Jeremiah Elvis Mercer," the mayor continued. He glanced around the office. "Where's your boy?"

The sheriff set the warrant down on his desk, then hoisted his gun belt. I had a fleeting sense he might pull out his gun and shoot Ellington right then and there. Instead, he came out from behind his desk, and ignoring the mayor, said to Sheriff Locke, "I'll get him."

He walked slowly into the back, which housed two jail cells, a meeting room, and a small bathroom.

The mayor rocked on his heels while waiting for Locke to make the arrest. Sheriff Locke stood stiffly, her gaze averted. I headed for the back to see what I could do to ease the sheriff's pain and assist Miah.

I found Sheriff Mercer standing in the small conference room, staring at the back door. The door stood open.

Sheriff Mercer turned to face me, his eyes rimmed again with tears.

"He's...gone."

"What evidence do they have?" Dan said over mochas at the Nugget.

"The mayor got a warrant to search Miah's comic book store. They found something."

"What? Evil comics?"

"Potassium chloride."

"Shit. I don't know that much about that stuff, but I know it can kill you. And it's not difficult to get. Especially if you work at a hospital." Dan took a sip of his mocha. "What made them search the place?"

"Anonymous tip," I said. I pushed the mocha away, too upset to add more acid to my stomach.

"Shit."

"No shit."

I was about to get up when I noticed everyone in the café was turned toward the front door. Everyone but me. I twisted around in my seat to see Mayor Ellington standing at the front entrance with Sheriff Locke by his side. In his hand he held up a water glass and a spoon. Apparently he'd been banging them together.

"...anyone seen Jeremiah Mercer?" I caught him mid-announcement. "We have issued a warrant for his arrest. If you are in any way assisting him, you are breaking the—"

Sheriff Locke took the glass and spoon away from the mayor and set them down on the nearby counter. "I'll handle this, Mayor." She gave him a look, and he stepped back. "Like the mayor said, we're looking for Jeremiah Mercer. If you've seen him, we'd appreciate your help in finding him. It's for his own safety."

Nobody said anything. I was tempted to, but a glance from Dan kept me from opening my big mouth.

"Now go on about your business," Sheriff Locke continued. "Sorry for the interruption." The two sat down at the counter as the Nugget patrons returned to their meatloafs and Cornish pasties and beer.

"That does it," I mumbled. "We've got to find the asshole that did this." I got out my notebook from my backpack and wrote a big question mark at the top of the page.

"What are you doing?" Dan asked, after tapping my note-book to get my attention.

"Making a list."

"Groceries or to-do?"

"Killers."

I started with the person who most deserved the chair and wrote: *Mayor Elijah Ellington.*

"You're not serious!" Dan said.

"Why not? This could all be a big smoke screen. He could easily be the killer and everyone would think he's above sus-picion."

"But what motive would he have? He'd be losing a voter. No politician would kill off a voter."

"Maybe he did it just to give the Jubilee all this attention. Maybe he's pretending to worry about the negative publicity when in fact it's exactly what he wants!"

"Connor, you really think the mayor would kill a Jubilee contestant just to sell a few more tickets? Pretty far-fetched, don't you think?"

"I'm happy with it," I said, and underlined the mayor's name. "Besides, people in small towns like this one always have plenty of far-fetched secrets. Ever watch those Aaron Spelling nighttime soaps? It's certainly possible that Mayor Ellington is...gay...and was having a torrid affair with... Da-kota when suddenly Dakota...changed his mind and dumped him for Simonie...."

"When in fact, the mayor is actually Dakota's real brother —sister?—separated at birth, just out of a coma, and had a sex-change operation—"

"You got any other suggestions?"

Dan shook his head, more like, "Connor, you're nuts" rather than, "No, I don't have any suggestions."

"Okay, how about Simonie, Dakota's girlfriend?"

Dan shrugged and sipped his mocha. "Did she have a motive?"

"Probably. Don't all women have motives for murdering

their men? Get us at the wrong time of the month, and wham."
I thought I saw Dan shiver in spite of the mocha. "Maybe he
was going to break up with her, and she didn't like that. Or
maybe she found out something about him and threatened to
blackmail him."

"The point is, Connor, there could be any number of reasons. How are we supposed to find out? Simonie's not going
to come pouring her secrets out to you. That's why they call
them 'secrets.'"

I had some witty repartee lined up, but instead I used some
informal sign language—I stuck my tongue out at him. "Yeah,
well, if we can find out her secret, we might just have a motive."

"That's a big 'if.'"

"All right, what about Holly, his ex? She's raising his son,
after being abandoned by him. She certainly has motive,
wouldn't you say?"

"I suppose. But what good would it do to kill Dakota? It
doesn't get him back as a boyfriend, and it doesn't get her a
father for her baby. If she did it out of revenge, he's not around
to suffer. Wouldn't it have been better to kill Simonie, if that
were the case?"

"Maybe she did try to kill Simonie and killed Dakota by accident. Maybe the poison was meant for her!"

"According to your logic, anything is possible. The way I
hear it over at the hospital, there were probably half a dozen
nurses on staff who didn't seem to mind that Dakota was
dead. What's up with that? And what about all those frog jockeys competing against Dakota? Miah wasn't the only one who
wanted to win that contest. But all these wild accusations sure
don't help us narrow down the field. Or help Miah."

I sank deeper into the red leatherette booth. "You're right.
It's just that I feel so helpless. And I have no real suspects. All
I know is, Miah didn't do it. So someone must have had a
grudge against Miah as well as Dakota, to kill one and frame
the other. That narrows it down a bit."

"To who?"

I glanced over at the counter where Mayor Ellington sat chatting with Sheriff Locke. He had a silly grin on his face and was leaning in toward the sheriff as if he were sharing something very private—even intimate—with her.

Oh my God! The man was flirting with Sheriff Mercer's woman!

I broke my pencil lead trying to triple-underline his name.

Chapter 16

I LEFT DAN at the café, eager to pursue a couple of possibilities, and drove over to Mother Lode Memorial. My first stop was ICU to check on Del Ores. Peering through the window, I saw Del Rey asleep in a chair next to her sister's bed. Del Ores slept, too, connected to machines that blinked red and green and white. I assumed the blinking was a good thing and moved away without disturbing them.

My next stop was Geriatrics, where I hoped to find Simonie on duty. She was nowhere in sight, and no one had seen her all morning even though she'd been scheduled to work.

"She probably took the day off," said one nurse, whose nameplate read JENNIFER REY. She stuck her pen in her mouth, which made her harder to read. Deaf people only catch forty to sixty percent of the speech they read, and we guess at the rest. When a mouth is obscured by gum, chewing tobacco, a mustache, or a pen, it makes for very challenging lipreading. "Her boyfriend was killed. Can't really blame her for being upset, even if Dakota was a jerk."

"You didn't like him?"

"He thought he was God's gift. All the new nurses fell for him at first when he laid on that charm. Then after a few weeks, after you got to know him better, you realized what a taker he really was."

"A taker?"

"Yeah, you know. He took, never gave."

"What did he take?"

"Anything he could get," said Nurse Jennifer, then left to answer a call.

Next I headed for Holly's ward to see if she could add a little insight to my list of suspects. Naturally, I wouldn't tell her she was on the list, too. Might be counterproductive. I found Holly in the cafeteria, thanks to another nurse who redirected me there.

"Holly!" I waved and approached her table where she sat alone, halfheartedly nibbling on rabbit food. She glanced up, expressionless. I sat down opposite her.

"Glad I caught up with you. I have a couple of questions I need to ask you."

Holly stuck a carrot in her mouth. I think she said, "What?"

"First of all, thanks for putting that envelope in my car."

"What envelope?" She showed no reaction.

Aha. So she was going to play that game. "Never mind. But thanks. Anyway, what I wanted to ask you was, is there any-one you can think of who might want Dakota dead?"

"You mean, besides me?" She stuck a piece of celery in her mouth.

"I...didn't mean..."

Luckily she removed the celery before she went on. "Look. I'm an obvious suspect, once you get past Miah. I hated him, too. He left me. He abandoned my child. He was a self-serving, egotistical bastard. I guess you could say I have a motive."

"So, did you kill him?" Deaf people tend to take the direct approach.

"Nope, someone beat me to it." She grinned. She had a tiny piece of carrot stuck between two teeth.

"So who do you think could have done it?"

"My bet's on Simonie."

"Really! But she loved him."

"Ah, but did she?" Holly glanced around the cafeteria, then met my eyes again.

"What do you mean?"

She shrugged. "I mean, maybe he was about to do to her what he did to me."

"You think he was about to dump her?"

"Or worse."

"What do you mean, worse?"

Holly chewed on a lettuce leaf for a moment, then she leaned in and spoke with exaggerated lip movements. "Let's just say, Dakota had a certain amount of power over some people. And he liked to play with it."

Remembering what Nurse Jennifer had implied, I said, "You mean, he was attractive. And a lot of the nurses here fell for him?"

"That was just the beginning. It was after that."

"I'm sorry. I just don't follow. What do you mean? Was he cheating on Simonie? Was he sleeping with a lot of women at the same time? What?"

Holly looked at her watch. "I've got to get back to work." She checked the room again, as if expecting someone.

"Wait!" As she began to lift her tray, I placed my hand on her arm. "Please. Tell me what you mean. There's a warrant out for Miah's arrest. He didn't do it. And I want to help him. If you know anything…"

Holly sighed. "Look, Dakota used his charm…for other purposes. He…let's just say, he had access to things at the hospital that other people wanted. And he made sure they wanted them. That's how he kept control."

"I don't—"

She stood up. "I'm sorry. I've already said too much. If any-one finds out I've been talking in a negative way about the hospital, I could be fired. I have to go."

She left me sitting there, staring at a green pea that had rolled off her veggie plate. It was perfectly round, green as an emerald, and ready to pop into someone's mouth. I touched it with a knife that had been left behind. The pea rolled to the edge of the table and stopped.

What did she mean by "talking about the hospital"? I thought we'd been discussing Dakota. What did Dakota have access to that could make him so popular—and then so hated?

I looked at the pea. Perched there at the edge of the table without the veggie plate context, it looked like one of my vitamin pills.

And then I knew what Dakota Webster had been up to. And why he was loved—and hated. And why the chemicals had been found in the creek. And probably why he was dead.

But I still didn't know who killed him.

I returned to the office to do a little more work at my day job— preparing for next week's newspaper, but my heart, and mind, weren't into it. My thoughts were taken up by visions of Del Ores in the hospital—and Dakota in the creek. Not to mention the possibility of Miah in a jail cell.

So Dakota was a drug source. He certainly had opportunity to get the drugs he wanted, hanging around the hospital all day. With help—from Simonie?—he could probably get whatever he needed, or needed to sell. Was he a druggie himself? If he were, surely it would turn up in Dr. Jackson's toxicology report.

Odd, I thought, that Dakota was drowned in contaminated water. Why wasn't he just stabbed, or poisoned through his food or drink? I'm sure anyone at the hospital would have access to him there, in one way or another. Why take the trouble—and risk—to drown him in the creek?

Poetic justice? Were killers that concerned about the arts?

The fact that Dakota croaked in the creek was just too much of a coincidence for me. That, and all those drugs floating around in the water. Did Dakota dump his excess supply there—and perhaps more? Why would he do that and risk the frog population? Was that part of his plan?

And where was Miah?

Nothing made sense. I decided to focus on Del Ores for a while and get my mind off the murder. Maybe something fresh would come if I concentrated on a different problem, and sometimes the solution to one problem helps with the solution to another. At least, it worked when I was having a newspaper publication problem. But then, that was just a deadline, not life and death.

I logged onto Yahoo, found my bookmark for GetWell, and reread the information listed at their website. Nothing new. Nothing surprising. No mystery—or solutions—here.

I backed up to the search engine and located the people search, then entered the name "Carrie Yates." All it gave me was a phone number and address and e-mail information. Same with Burnett Pike. I logged off and headed for Dan's office.

"You're a hot-shot P.I.," I said, finding Dan resting his feet on his desk and reading a file.

"That I am," Dan said. "Anyone you want found, photographed, spied on, overheard, followed, bio'd, or compromised, I'm your man."

"You're my man anyway. Or have you forgotten?"

"Couldn't forget a thing like that. I was thinking about it just now." He grinned.

I blushed. "I thought you were reading a file."

"It's a fake file. Like in school, when we used to hold up those world history textbooks, and we were really reading *Mad* magazine. It's my Fantasy File."

"Stop. You're getting me hot. I've got a job for you."

"How much does it pay?"

"I only pay in sex."

"I'm your man."

"Let's not go through this again. Can you find out some information on Carrie Yates and Burnett Pike for me?"

"Piece of cake." He pulled his feet from the desk and logged onto his computer. The *Star Wars* screen saver melted into a search engine I didn't recognize.

"What's that? I don't recognize it."

"Secret search engine. Only for professionals, like me."

"Cute," I said, sitting on the edge of his desk to watch the professional at work.

He hunted-and-pecked a bunch of letters, and in minutes the screen filled with all kinds of data. I scanned the information, looking for something I recognized. Finally a name appeared, along with a list of public and private records.

NAME: Catherine Pauline Yates
DOB: 4/11/45
BIRTHPLACE: Mother Lode Memorial Hospital, Sonora CA

The information went on to list her education—graduated from Mark Twain High School, no college mentioned; marital status—married twenty years to Monko Yates, then six months to Burnett Pike; property ownership—the GetWell, BeWell, etc., centers; medical history—healthy until recently. In the last six months she'd been admitted to MLMH four times with an undiagnosed illness. Finally her credit information appeared—clean except for a couple of late payments about the time Monko died.

"How do you get all this stuff?" I asked.

"Want more?"

"Like what?"

"If I look hard enough—and know where to look—I can tell you her toothpaste brand, what size bra she wears, her last vacation spot, her financial status, even her favorite color. I can probably tell you everything about her except what she's thinking right now."

"My God, that's incredible. You can do that for anyone?"

"Like I said, if you know where to look and how to get in, it's a piece of cake."

I thought for a moment, then looked at Dan directly and said, "What toothpaste brand do I buy?"

"Crest. With whiteners and baking soda and fluoride."

"Too easy. You saw it on my bathroom counter. What's my favorite color?"

"Yellow."

I gasped. "How did you know? Other than my underwear, I never wear yellow!"

"But it is your favorite color, right?"

"Yes... Do I talk in my sleep?"

Dan punched a few keys and another screen filled with information appeared. This time my name was at the top. After a long list of my public and private information, my Victoria's Secret bill appeared. The words seemed to scream, "Look at me!" I blushed. There, in LED, for all the world—and Dan—to read, was the documentation of my latest underwear purchases. Two yellow bras and two pairs of yellow underpants. And the price. And the size. Where my underwear came from was nobody's business!

"Turn that off!" I said, reaching for the keyboard.

"Just showing you what you can find on a computer these days. Pretty impressive, isn't it?"

"It's downright scary! You know way too much about me."

"Not really. There's still a lot up there I haven't figured out yet." He pointed to my head.

"Well, it's not for publication. In the meantime, stick to the matter at hand. Can you pull up information on Burnett Pike?"

"Like I said, piece of cake." He turned back to the computer and typed in the letters: "B-u-r-n-e-t-t P-i-k-e."

After a few seconds, the screen uploaded a bunch of crazy symbols, then stopped. Dan scrolled down the page to find the word: "NAME:"

The line was blank.

And so was the rest of the list.

In the search box blinked the words, "File not found."

Chapter 17

"THAT'S INTERESTING," Dan said. He punched a few more keys, tried a couple of other searches, and still came up with nothing.

"Not his real name?" I asked.

"Possibly."

I slipped off the edge of Dan's desk. "I think I'll pay him another visit. I'm hoping to get my Uncle Danny in there, remember? He's senile, you know."

"Thanks a lot."

"It was the only name I could think of under stress."

"I'm flattered."

Back at my office, I did some sleuthing the old-fashioned way—the phone. I called up the local county recorder's office via my TTY, hoping someone might be working over the weekend. Not many private services or agencies have teletypewriters for the deaf, but most government offices are required to have them. Only trouble is, many of the staff don't know how to use them. I got lucky this time; a man who identified himself as S-H-E-L-D-O-N S-I-E-G-E-L answered the phone.

"HELLO SHELDON," I typed in all caps, the standard format for TTY use. "CONNOR WESTPHAL, PUBLISHER OF THE *EUREKA!* NEWSPAPER HERE. I HAVE A COUPLE OF QUESTIONS I'D LIKE TO ASK YOU. GA" I gave the "Go ahead," hoping he'd know what it meant.

"THAT'S WHAT I'M HERE FOR. HOW CAN I HELP YOU? GA"

"I NEED SOME DATA ON A CITIZEN, NAME: BURNETT PIKE. DO YOU HAVE DOB, MARRIAGE LICENSE, ANYTHING OF PUBLIC RECORD? GA"

"HOLD ON..."

I retyped a short article on the computer while I waited for Sheldon Siegel to return. After about five minutes, the red glow of words began to dance across the small TTY screen.

"GOT A MARRIAGE LICENSE FOR A BURNETT NMN PIKE. MARRIED ONE CATHERINE PAULINE YATES, DATED SIX MONTHS AGO, COUNTY OF CALAVERAS. THIS WHAT YOU WANT? GA"

"YES, THANKS. DOES IT LIST HIS DOB OR ANYTHING ELSE? GA"

"BORN IN 1955, DAYTONA BEACH, FL. GA"

"ANYTHING ELSE? GA"

"NOTHING MORE. EXCEPT OWNERSHIP OF PROPERTY. YOU WANT THAT INFO? GA"

"YES, PLEASE. SPECIFICALLY, DOES HE OWN THE GETWELL CENTER IN FLAT SKUNK? GA"

There was a long pause, then, "YES. TOOK OWNERSHIP ABOUT SIX MONTHS AGO. CO-OWNS WITH CATHERINE YATES, WHO FORMERLY OWNED THE PLACE WITH ONE MONKO YATES. GA"

"THANKS SO MUCH. YOU'VE BEEN A GREAT HELP! GA SK" I typed the code for "Stop keying," to let him know I was finished. For a few seconds there was no "SK" in response. Thinking he might have forgotten to formally wrap up the conversation, I was about to hang up when a few words popped up on the screen.

"ONE MORE THING, IN CASE IT'S IMPORTANT. THIS BURNETT PIKE ALSO OWNS A NUMBER OF OTHER PROPERTIES. OF ANY INTEREST TO YOU? GA"

Other properties? "YES, WHAT DO YOU HAVE? GA"

"ACCORDING TO PUBLIC RECORDS, HE AND THIS CATHERINE YATES OWN THREE OTHER BUSINESSES: BEWELL, STAYWELL, LIVE-WELL, ALL LOCATED IN THE MOTHER LODE AREA, FROM SUTTER'S MILL TO PLACERVILLE. GA"

Not surprising, but still disconcerting. A chain of health

care centers. All belonging to the newlywed Burnett Pike, after
the demise of Monko Yates and marriage to Carrie Yates. A
nice little business.

"THANKS AGAIN, MR. SIEGEL. I OWE YOU ONE. GA SK"

"YOU PUBLISH THE EUREKA? HOW ABOUT A NICE ARTICLE ON
THE SELFLESS WAY YOUR GOVERNMENT SERVES THE PUBLIC?
<GRIN> GA SK."

Not a bad idea, I thought, temporarily forgetting the doz-
ens of times the bureaucracy of the same government drove
me crazy. Seemed as if Sheldon Siegel enjoyed his job. I wondered how much Burnett Pike enjoyed his new businesses.
The ones he'd acquired by marriage.

By the time I hung up the phone, it was nearly dinnertime. I
grabbed a quick Cornish pasty from DILLIGAF's (Does-It-
Look-Like-I-Give-a-Fuck) deli and ate as I drove back to the
GetWell Center. When I pulled up, they'd left a light on for me.
In fact, they'd left most of the lights in the front of the house
on. Probably didn't worry about their utility bills, what with all
that Medicare money coming in.

As I approached the door, I tried to think of something sad
to conjure up the right demeanor for my next interview with
Burnett Pike. I knew he was growing tired of me and my questions, so I had to have a good reason for dropping by yet a
third time in one day.

I stood poised at the door, ready to knock, and thought
about the most devastating thing I could come up with: What
if there were no more chocolate in the world?

Tears came to my eyes.

I knocked.

After a few seconds, Burnett Pike answered the door, looking tired and frazzled. He said nothing in the way of greeting,
just stared at me as if he had no idea why I was there.

"I'm sorry, Mr. Pike. I...I didn't know where else to go. It's
my uncle—he's worse. I'm afraid I may have to move him in

here tomorrow. You seemed like someone I could talk to. Do you mind if I come in for a minute?" No more chocolate. No more chocolate. A few more tears appeared.

Burnett Pike stammered. "I...I'm terribly busy...."

I blinked and almost managed to squeeze out a drop. He probably thought I was winking at him.

"All right, come in for a moment. But I must get my wife ready for bed."

I glanced at my watch as he turned to allow me inside. Six-thirty. A little early for bed.

"What's the problem, Ms...."

"Westphal. My Uncle Danny, he's taken a turn for the worse." God, at least if I was going to play the actress, I could come up with some better lines. "But I'm worried about transporting him all the way here from Sutter's Mill. That's where he lives."

"We have a center there, too. What seems to be wrong with him now?"

I hadn't thought that far ahead. When lying, I like to stay generic. The more details I give, the more chance I have of slipping up. "I don't know what the doctors call it. But I know he's worse. Ever since he moved here from Florida, he's gotten weaker and weaker."

I watched Burnett Pike for any sign of recognition of the state. Bingo! His eyes narrowed and his lips tightened.

"It was just too far away for us to care for him, you know? Have you ever been to Florida, Mr. Pike?"

"Uh, no, can't say that I have."

I blinked. Had I read his lips correctly?

"Really? I understand it's beautiful there."

"Yes, I'm sure it is. But your uncle needs to be near the family. And now it appears he needs professional care. We can transfer him in tomorrow after you fill out the proper forms. I'll get them."

When he stepped out of the room, I stood up and took a quick walk to the NO ADMITTANCE supply room door to see if it might have been left unlocked. No such luck. The medications were all tucked away, safe from the prying eyes of Connor Westphal.

I returned to the lobby to see if anything out of the ordinary jumped out at me. Most of the furniture and knickknacks had a feminine touch. Nothing seemed like it might have come from Burnett Pike. When he returned in a few minutes with a handful of forms, I asked him about the one thing in the room that might lead to more questions.

"Is this your wedding photo?" I asked, picking it up from the mantel. A mismatched pair if I ever saw one.

He nodded and took the photo from me, replacing it on the mantel. "Just fill these out and we'll take care of everything. He's on Medicare, I assume."

That clever line of questioning went nowhere. I had to think fast or I'd be out the door without a paddle.

"Oh, thank you. I'm so relieved, Mr. Pike...you know, that name sounds familiar. Are you a relative of Jeremiah Pike from Poker Flat?"

"No, no relation."

"Where did you grow up?"

"All over, really. We moved around a lot."

"So your family wasn't from around here? I'm a bit of a historian. I love to learn about people's backgrounds."

"I was adopted, so I don't know much about my heritage. Don't even know my exact birthday."

"Wow!" I said. And, Wow! I thought. What a liar. "What a sad story."

"I'm used to it, believe me. Now you'll have to excuse me. I'll see you and your uncle tomorrow."

"Thanks so much for caring," I said, nearly choking on the word. "Good night."

Burnett Pike—or whoever he was—closed the door without saying good-bye. And I was up the creek...with a dead body and no viable suspects. Except for the fact that the Mother Lode Memorial Hospital wasn't the only place that housed a lot of medications like those found in Critter's Creek. So did GetWell Health Care Center.

It was dark by the time I left the center. I drove on to Mother Lode Memorial, hoping this time I'd catch Simonie so I could ask her a few questions. The nurse on duty had said she'd be back for a split shift that evening to make up for her absence in the middle of the day. Unless, of course, she'd disappeared...

But she hadn't. I found her on the geriatrics floor, reading a magazine behind the nurses' desk. Makeup applied, every hair in place, she didn't look too bad for a woman who was mourning the loss of her boyfriend. She looked up from her reading—or the pictures anyway—and asked, "What do you want?"

I hate people who beat around the bush. "I want to talk to you about Dakota."

"He's dead. And I know which side you're on. You're trying to protect Miah, saying he didn't do it. Well, you're wrong."

My strategy in a situation like this is simple: When you have nothing else to say, act like you do.

"I know what's been going on around here."

"What do you mean?" The muscles in her neck tensed as she spoke.

I took a chance—and kept it simple. "The drugs."

She blinked several times and pressed her lips together, as if trying to keep herself from speaking. It was clear from her body language that I had hit a nerve. "I don't know what you're—"

"Cut the crap, Simonie. I know all about the drugs. Now, I can go to the sheriff and have him start a full-out investigation, or you can tell me what I need to know to help clear Miah. You know as well as I do that he's not capable of murder. That leaves you as a primary suspect, in my opinion. And I'll share that opinion with Sheriff Mercer, along with what I know about the drugs, if you don't start talking to me."

Simonie glanced around to see if anyone could overhear us. I never worry about that, but hearing people seem to be obsessed with it, especially when it's something personal. "Shut up, will you! Jeez!"

She came out from behind the desk and pulled me into an unoccupied hospital room. Flipping on the light, she closed the door behind us and turned to face me, arms crossed in front of her, eyes wild with anger. Or fear?

"You want to get me fired? That's all I need right now!"

"So tell me what's up."

She plopped on the neatly made bed and began picking at the nibs on the hospital-issue bedspread. "It was Dakota."

I waited, then urged her on. "Dakota?"

She nodded. Her dirty-blond hair, once perfect, now fell across her face. She brushed it aside and met my eyes. "He...supplied it. He had access, you know, and I needed it...."

I glanced at her arms. They were covered in long sleeves. I'd never seen her bare arms and wondered if she kept them hidden. She caught me looking.

"I don't shoot. Nothing shows. I'm too careful for that."

"What are you on?"

She shrugged. "Just stuff, you know. Anyway, Dakota got me hooked. We used to party a lot. Then he stopped giving it to me and told me I had to buy it, that he couldn't afford to keep me on it. So I started buying from him."

"You don't have access to drugs here at the hospital yourself?"

"God, no! We'd all be addicts if everyone had access."

"Then how did Dakota get the key?"

She forced a laugh. "The way he got everything. He slept with the nurse who had access and got a copy of her key."

"So he was a dealer."

She nodded.

"Was he on drugs himself?"

"I don't think so. He'd party a little but never seemed hooked, you know."

"Do you think he used some kind of drug on his frog? In order to win the contest?"

"I don't know. All I know is, he said he had a superfrog this year, and he wouldn't tell anyone the details. Said it was top secret."

"Do you think he put the drugs in the creek water to kill off the competition?"

"I have no idea, but I wouldn't put anything past him."

"I thought you were in love with him. You don't seem very upset about losing him after all that drama a while ago."

"I was pissed. I lost my connection."

"You didn't love him?"

She shrugged. I couldn't tell from the body language if she really cared or not.

"Was he about to break up with you?"

Simonie shot me a glance. "Who told you?"

Lucky guess. "I can't reveal my sources. But it does give you a motive for murder."

"I told you! He was my connection. I wouldn't kill him!"

"But he was about to drop you. That must have made you angry."

"I'm more pissed off about losing my connection than my boyfriend. And that hardly makes me a killer. I...I gotta get back to work."

She stood up from the bed and headed for the door. Turning back, she said, "You aren't going to tell anyone, are you? Confidential sources and all that, right?"

I said nothing.

"I don't want to lose my job."

"I don't think the patients would want you on the job under the influence."

"I'm not—not anymore. But if you say anything, I swear, I'll..." Her face turned red. She glared at me long and hard, then turned off the light and stalked out the door, leaving me in total darkness.

Chapter 18

I WONDERED IF Holly was still around. Figured I might as well kill two nurses with one shot. Bad metaphor.

"Is Holly Samuels still on duty?" I asked the nurse in ICU.

"No, she went home hours ago. Is there something I can do for you?"

I read her nameplate. "No thanks, Ms. Obregar. We were going to meet for dinner, but I guess she forgot." I tried to look disappointed.

"Sorry about that. Did you try the hospital café? She lives so close, she often eats here, since it's a lot cheaper than most restaurants. Worth a try, anyway."

I thanked Ms. Obregar and headed for the cafeteria. She was right—it was worth a try. Besides, I was getting hungry.

The Mother Lode Memorial Café was full when I entered. I searched the room for Holly's bushy dark hair but spotted only one person, back turned, who might fit the bill. This woman had a kid with her.

Then I remembered. Holly had a baby. Maybe it was her after all. As I wound my way through the room, the closer I got, the more I was convinced it was the woman I was looking for. But I caught the eye of the baby first.

"Gadda!" I think the baby said. He looked about a year old, but it was hard to tell under his mashed potato facial.

"Gadda!" I replied, hoping I hadn't said anything distasteful in baby language. The mother looked up.

"What are you doing here?" Holly said, another spoon of mashed potatoes ready for the baby's babbling mouth. She set the spoon down. The baby looked at it longingly.

"The nurse told me you might be here."

She picked up the spoon again. The baby opened his mouth expectantly. I sat down across from Holly.

"I've already told you everything I know."

"I just had a few more questions. Some things have come out, and I wondered what your take was."

She frowned and put the spoon down again. The baby watched it return to the plate. His lower lip quivered.

"Cute baby," I said.

"Thanks. He's a mess right now." She dabbed at his chin and cheeks but only managed to scrape the surface.

"What's his name?" I lifted the spoon still filled with mashed potatoes.

"Jonathan. He's named after my dad."

Jonathan opened his mouth in anticipation of the incoming food. I scooped it in like a professional and sat back, pleased with my mothering skills.

"Fffwwatt!"

I jumped back, feeling the wet sticky spray on my face. Jonathan had spit the potatoes back at me! The little bra—

"Sorry about that!" Holly said, but she didn't look sorry. She was trying to suppress a grin. "That means he likes you."

Yeah sure, I thought, grabbing a napkin from the holder. I wiped my face, forced a smile at Jonathan, and scooted my chair back from the armed and dangerous kid.

"Goody," I said. "Or he's mad that I interrupted his dinner."

Holly smiled and filled Jonathan's mouth with another dollop of white goo. "So what did you find out?"

"I talked with someone who seems to think Dakota was a drug dealer."

"Who?" Holly asked.

"I can't say, you know that. So, was he?"

"A dealer? I guess you could call it that. He got drugs for people. They paid for them. I guess that's drug dealing. Only it seemed different with him. It felt like he was just helping people get the drugs they needed. And it wasn't like he was a street dealer."

"Apparently not, since he got the stuff from the hospital pharmacy."

Holly's eyes lit up, just like her baby's when he was ready for another spoonful. For a moment there, I was afraid she was going to spit at me. "How did you find that out?"

I didn't answer. Instead I asked, "Did he supply you with drugs?"

Holly suddenly looked angry. "Of course not! I never take drugs. Not now, anyway."

"You did at one time?"

She hesitated, then said, "Before I got pregnant, I kind of partied a lot. You know. Then after Jonathan was born, I went through a big postpartum depression. Dakota got me something to help me. Zoloft. But I've been off it for a couple of months. Besides, it's not exactly a recreational drug, you know."

"But you also took drugs before you got pregnant."

"Just the usual stuff that goes around, and only at parties. I'm not a druggie."

"What did you take?"

"You know, this is really none of your business." Holly began to pack up her things. She stood, leaving the half-eaten trays of food on the table, and picked up Jonathan and the diaper bag.

"I'm sorry if it seems like I'm being nosy, Holly, but I have an idea Dakota's drug dealing may have something to do with his death."

"Well, I wouldn't know about that. And I think you're looking at the wrong motive. The person who killed Dakota hated him."

"How can you be so sure?"

" 'Cause I know, that's all. Why don't you ask Simonie?"
With that, she left the cafeteria.
And I was right behind her.

I followed Holly to her apartment, two blocks down from the hospital. I kept my distance, hoped I didn't walk too loudly, and watched her under the pale streetlights as she made her way up the outside staircase and disappeared behind a corner.

I didn't follow her up. All I wanted was to know where she lived, in case I needed to talk with her again. This wasn't the time. I'd done enough damage to last a couple of hours.

I went home to work for a while but couldn't keep my mind on future newspaper articles. All I could think about was Dakota and the various possible motives people might have had for killing him. Drug dealing. Revenge. Hatred. Scandal. Blackmail. The only thing missing was gluttony. I'd have to check his refrigerator and make sure that wasn't an option.

Around ten o'clock I had come up with another idea to discuss with Holly about the envelope she'd left in the car. I wondered if she'd be awake. Didn't matter. This couldn't wait.

I headed for her apartment, wishing I could call first and let her know I was coming, but I knew she wouldn't have a TTY. I'd just have to take a chance that she'd see me again. When I explained the reason, I was fairly certain she'd let me in.

I parked the Chevy and made my way up the apartment staircase, hoping I'd be able to recognize her unit from the others by finding some clue—a toy left outside, a stroller waiting, a nameplate that read HOLLY SAMUELS. The walkway was clean, except for a couple of newspapers lying on door-mats. Both of them were the *Eureka!,* apparently still un-read. I figured they weren't home. That let out two of the apartments.

I walked by the other three and studied the doors. One had

a NO SOLICITORS sticker on it. Not Holly's. With a baby, she wouldn't have time to fool with such organized warnings. One door sported a doormat covered with white cat hair. Holly didn't have cat hair on her. And she probably couldn't deal with a cat and a baby, too, being a single mother in a small apartment.

That left one apartment. B-5. I glanced around, hoping something would speak to me. I put my face to the door to check for vibrations of life inside, such as the TV set. I have a little bone-conductive sensation, but all it tells me is that something is turned on, not what the details might be.

I felt something. But not the intermittent vibrations of a loud TV. Instead I felt a thumping. Soft, repetitive, but not regular like a washing machine. I figured that at least she was awake.

I knocked. I waited. No answer. I knocked again, harder, longer. Nothing.

I tried to peek through a gap in the front window curtains, but all I could see was an empty living room area with the lights on. No sign of life.

Then, out of the corner of my eye, I saw something move. I strained to see what it was, but the room contained only an empty couch, a standing lamp, and a baby's crib. No people.

And then I realized it was the crib that was moving.

I watched it for several seconds and saw it move again. It slid half an inch on the loose rug. My hand was pressed against the door, and I felt a thump at the same time the crib bounced.

Jonathan must have been inside it.

So where was Holly? Using the blow dryer or taking a shower and unable to hear me? I pounded on the door for several minutes, but no one came to answer.

And no one entered the living room to check on Jonathan.

I was about to knock again when I saw another movement, this time inside the crib. A second later, Jonathan pulled himself up to standing, holding onto the slats. His back was to me, but I could see him reaching a hand out for something. I knocked on the door again. Slowly he turned to face the front window.

Tears streamed down his red face.

I pounded again but sensed it was useless. For whatever reason, Holly wasn't going to answer the door. I tried the knob.

I was stunned to find it was unlocked. That couldn't be good—but it was good for me.

I opened the door and quickly went to rescue the crying baby.

"It's okay, it's okay," I repeated, lifting Jonathan from his crib and holding him in my arms. I swung him gently from side to side to comfort him, but he continued crying. Then he reached an arm out toward the back room. Before I could move, I smelled something.

Gas.

Oh God!

I ran to the bedroom and turned the knob of the closed door. The knob turned but the door wouldn't open. Something was blocking it.

I ran from the apartment carrying the baby and pounded on the nearest neighbor's door. No answer. I ran to the next one and pounded again, screaming, "I need help!" An old man opened the door angrily. I didn't have time to read his lips or explain the details. I thrust Jonathan into his arms, yelled back, "Call 911—gas!" and returned to Holly's apartment.

Taking a deep breath before entering, I ran to the stove and switched off the gas. Then I ran to the bedroom door and pushed against it with all my strength. The door opened half an inch. I stood back, then rammed it again. My shoulder hurt like hell, and I only gained another half inch. Again and again I threw myself at the door, slowly inching it open. After a few more attempts I saw what was blocking the door.

Holly.

She lay sprawled on the floor, her back to the door. I shoved at her, trying to move her dead-weight bulk so I could get the door open. I forced myself not to breathe deeply, but the shallow breaths were taking their toll. I felt light-headed, nauseated, and dizzy. I ran outside, grabbed a huge breath, then returned to the task of moving Holly out of the way so I could get the door open.

After two more shoves, I managed to roll her over and open the door. She lay unconscious on the floor in her nightclothes. I grabbed her arms and began pulling her through the doorway, but her body seemed to catch on every obstacle—the doorjamb, the rug, the coffee table, the crib. Everything seemed to be trying to keep me from getting her out of that gas-filled apartment.

Just as I reached the front door, two firefighters burst in. One ran into the apartment, apparently to look for the source of the gas leak, while the other lifted Holly from the floor and took her outside, into the fresh oxygen-filled air.

As I stepped outside to get myself a new supply, I saw Jonathan, still being held by the old man, still crying. I took the baby into my arms, as my eyes filled with tears.

"Is she going to be all right?" I asked a paramedic working on Holly with an oxygen mask. I couldn't read his answer and looked to the old man for confirmation.

He nodded and said, "They're taking her to Memorial," as they whisked her away, leaving me holding her young son.

I looked at Jonathan and wiped his tears, then mine. "Mommy's going to be fine, sweetie, don't you worry."

How easy it is to lie to children, I thought. How easy it is for some people to lie to everyone.

Chapter 19

"CONNOR! WHAT happened here?"

Sheriff Mercer had arrived, along with Sheriff Locke, just as the paramedics were leaving. I still held the baby, and we had both managed to stop crying.

"I...came over...the lights were on...I felt something...the door was unlocked...."

Sheriff Mercer had his hand raised about halfway through my rant. "Hold on! Hold on! You're not making any sense. Not that that's unusual. Start over."

I did, and I think I was more coherent. Until the ending. Then his eyes started rolling again.

"So you just happened by here, for no particular reason—"

"I had a reason!"

"What?"

I stared at him. For the life of me, I couldn't remember why I'd come. The trauma of finding Holly had pushed it right out of my mind. "I wanted to...ask her something."

"Connor, are you holding something back? 'Cause if you are—"

"No, Sheriff, I just can't remember right now, honestly. It's been a little traumatic. But I will. And I'll tell you everything I know. I just need some time to clear my mind, okay?"

The sheriff nodded reluctantly and moved away to talk with someone on his cell phone. Sheriff Locke kept the accumulating neighbors at bay while the firefighters stood around discussing why the burner was on but not lit. I lip-read snatches of conversation until I saw another car drive up. A woman stepped out, carrying a large bag. I had a hunch who it was as she made her way up the stairs.

The woman was neatly dressed but with disheveled hair, as if she might have been sleeping. She headed for Sheriff Locke, asked her a question, then the sheriff nodded in my direction. I held Jonathan a little tighter as the woman approached.

"Ms. Westphal?" She smiled and reached out a hand. "I'm Victoria Serpa. I work for county social services. Someone placed a call to our office."

I nodded, shook her hand while balancing the baby on one hip, then wrapped my arm back around him.

"Is this the baby?"

"Yes, Jonathan Samuels. At least, I think that's his last name. His mother is Holly Samuels, a nurse over at Mother Lode Memorial. She's there now."

"I overheard something about a drug overdose?"

"No!" I said, a little too strongly. "No, she...passed out from exposure to a gas leak."

"Suicide attempt?"

"No! I'm sure you've got this all wrong. It was an accident, I'm sure. I called you because I wanted someone to come and take care of the baby while Holly's in the hospital. It's not going to be anything permanent." I found myself holding Jonathan tighter again.

"These are just standard questions, Ms. Westphal. Most of our cases are drug-related. Some are suicide. She has no living relatives?"

"I don't know. You'll have to check. I just happened to be here and found her unconscious. I got the baby out...."

"You did the right thing." She reached for Jonathan.

I held back.

"Where are you going to take him?" I looked at his big blue eyes, then back at her tiny brown ones.

"We'll put him in foster care until the mother is...fit."

I didn't like the way she said "fit."

"We have several families willing to take infants in emergency situations like this. He'll be well cared for." She reached for Jonathan again, and I slowly moved him toward her. He clung to me and began sniffling again.

"He doesn't seem to want to go."

Victoria Serpa continued to hold her arms open for the baby. "He'll be fine. Come to me, Johnny," she said to him.

"His name is Jonathan." I unpeeled his legs, wrapped tightly around my waist, and tried again to move him into the social worker's arms. He began to scream.

Victoria Serpa took him firmly but gently from me, talking to him even as he screamed. The firefighters and sheriffs looked over—the baby must have been causing quite a racket—but the social worker seemed unaffected by his terror. She just kept smiling and talking to him. Finally, she turned to go. I touched her on the shoulder.

"Where can I find him?"

"I'm afraid you can't. We keep our placements confidential to protect the child. We'll be contacting the mother about his placement though."

"Why do you need to protect the child?"

"You never know. Until we find out exactly what happened to the mother, there could be other factors involved. Such as the father, and what role he plays in this."

"The father is dead," I said bluntly, watching for her reaction.

That smile never wavered. She'd heard it all. "Nevertheless, it's government policy. We have only the child's best interests in mind."

With that, she whisked the baby down the stairs, into the car seat waiting for him, and away from his home.

"You can't go in there," Sheriff Mercer said, as I took a step into the apartment.

"Why not?"

"You know the rule, C.W. I got to investigate it first. See if I can figure out what happened here. Consider it a crime scene, understand?"

"But I was just in there. I've already contaminated it if that's what you're worried about."

"Sorry, C.W., it's off limits. You wanna wait and see what we find, that's okay. But you can't go in. Not until we're done, anyway. Got it?"

"I got it! I got it! Jeez."

As the sheriffs entered the apartment, I glanced up and down the apartment walkway, not exactly sure what to do with myself. I could wait for results of the crime scene investigation, which could take hours. Or I could go home and go to bed.

Or I could go to the hospital and try to find out what happened to Holly.

"Sheriff?" I called into the apartment, careful not to set foot inside.

In a few seconds, the sheriff appeared in the living room. He was on his cell phone again. I waited for him to finish the call.

When he hung up, he frowned at me. Before he had a chance to bawl me out for interrupting his evidence search, I said, "I'm going over to the hospital to see if Holly's awake. Will you let me know if you find anything here?"

Sheriff Mercer shook his head.

"Why not?"

"Why not what?"

Apparently he hadn't been listening. Or his hearing aid wasn't turned on. "I said, I'm going to the hospital to see what happened to Holly. Will you let me know if you find anything here?"

"Already did," he said cryptically.

"What do you mean?"

"I mean, I know what happened to Holly. You don't need to go to the hospital."

"She was overcome by the gas."

He shook his head. "That's not why she was unconscious."

I thought about the baby. Jonathan hadn't been unconscious, only Holly. And she was in the next room, farther from the gas than Jonathan.

"What happened, then?"

"She OD'd."

That's not possible, I thought, as I drove to the hospital. Holly said she didn't do drugs. Anymore.

So maybe she was a liar, I answered back. People don't like to share their drug addiction secrets with virtual strangers.

But I would have noticed, I argued. I'm good at things like that. I read body language. She wasn't lying. And she wasn't doing drugs.

Drug addicts get very good at disguising their habits, I begged to differ.

This conversation with myself went on for the entire drive. When I arrived at the hospital parking lot, neither one of us had won the debate. I headed into the emergency room, hoping for an answer.

"Holly Samuels. Where is she?" I demanded of the nurse who stopped me at the door to the ER.

"You can't go in there. See the volunteer at the desk."

I backed off, knowing it was futile to have an argument with a nurse when I couldn't even win an argument with myself. I headed for the main reception desk and found a volunteer just waiting to answer my question. Holly was in the Intensive Care Unit. The same floor as Del Ores.

"Visiting hours are over," a nurse said, as she passed me in the hall. "Didn't you hear the PA announcement?"

I shook my head, tapped my ear, and shrugged.

She mouthed the words like a cartoon character. "Vis-it-ing-hours-are-ov-er." She shook her head, tapped her watch, but didn't shrug.

"Thank-you," I aped back, then turned and pretended to head for the elevators. Peering around the corner, I watched as the nurse walked away. Probably occupied with hunting down after-hours visitors throughout the hospital.

I sneaked back down the hall and peeked into the first room I came to. An old man in an oxygen tent. I shivered and let the door close softly. I tried two more rooms—both empty, thank God—and finally found Holly in the next room.

She was hooked up to an IV, a monitor of some kind, and a machine that looked like something from a *Star Wars* space-ship. I started to get a closer look when a light shaft from the door struck the floor.

I ducked under the bed, just in time to watch a pair of white nurse's shoes enter the room. Staying in character, I duck-walked farther under Holly's high hospital bed and curled up into a ball.

The nurse fooled around with a bunch of stuff I couldn't see and finally left the room after maybe five minutes. I crawled out from under the bed, tried to stand, and got a crick in my neck. I moved up slowly, rubbing my neck as I stretched.

Holly looked the same. So did the monitors, but the IV looked full. And Holly's pillow had been fluffed. I pulled her chart from the end of the bed and took it over to the dim hospital night-light.

The first few pages were mostly chicken scratches. Doctors learn a different type of handwriting when they get to medical school. They have to unlearn all those perfect T's and curling O's and learn to write in zigzag. It was much like reading lips—I could make out only the occasional word and had to piece together the rest. The medications were all written in secret pharmaceutical code. I copied down some of the marks in my notebook and replaced the chart.

I stroked Holly's IV-free hand and told her her son was fine and that everything was going to be all right. She didn't respond.

I left the room, wondering if I'd just lied to her—and myself.

Chapter 20

ALL NIGHT LONG I dreamt about frogs. Frogs that talked. Frogs that wore clothes. Frogs that ran a newspaper called the *Euribbet!* I even dreamt about evil frogs who poisoned the meatloaf at the Nugget Café. Frogs.

I woke up with a start when my Shake-Awake alarm went off at 6:30. Early for a Sunday. But not when there was a festival in town that seemed to produce dead bodies—both amphibious and human.

If you could call Dakota Webster human. He was beginning to sound more like a toad.

My first thought, lying in my sofabed, was of Jonathan. I wondered how he'd fared the night. Then I thought of Holly and wondered if she was alert. I lay under my cozy comforter for another ten minutes, trying to figure out how many lives Dakota Webster had affected in some negative way. Holly had been unceremoniously dumped by him. Jonathan had been abandoned by him. Simonie had been introduced to drugs because of him. And Miah was about to be arrested, thanks to him.

My phone light flashed, forcing me out of my thoughts and out of my bed.

"HELLO?" I typed into the TTY, adding the standard GA.

"Good morning, Beautiful. GA"

I recognized Dan's greeting. And he typed in standard lowercase, like most hearing people who don't communicate with

164

many deaf people. "What are you doing up at this hour? GA" I typed back.

"Wondering if you're heading for the Jubilee this morning? They're having a Pancake Breakfast. All you can eat. Blueberry with maple syrup. Hungry? GA"

I wasn't until he started typing words like pancakes and blueberry and syrup. "I am now. Pick me up? GA"

"Will do. Got an idea for you. GA"

"What? See how fat I can get in one morning? GA"

"How's your Hangtown Fry? GA"

Hangtown Fry? I made the classic Gold Country dish only on special occasions, and I used my own version of the recipe, substituting shrimp for the oysters, pancetta for the bacon, and rigatoni for the scrambled eggs.

"Why? GA"

"I'll tell you over a heap of hotcakes. See you in an hour. GA KS KS."

That was Dan, all right. I'd once mistaken a call from a killer as Dan, but now that he had his own personalized sign-off, I wouldn't make that mistake again. Instead of using SK for "Stop keying," he reversed the letters and signed off with KS...for "Kiss." Isn't he the sweetest?

After a homemade mocha and a shower, I pulled on my most comfortable jeans and a top that read: IF YOU CAN READ THIS, YOU'RE TOO CLOSE. I fed Casper, then roughhoused with her until we were both panting, and one of us was drooling. I thought about bringing her along to the Jubilee, but with all those frogs hopping around, the temptation for a snack would be too much for my Siberian husky.

Casper suddenly began barking. I had a hunch I knew what she was trying to tell me. Dan had arrived—she knew the sound of his car. I opened the front door, waved, grabbed my backpack, and headed over to the car.

"Been working up an appetite?" Dan leaned over and opened the passenger door from the inside.

I wiped a few beads of sweat from my forehead. "It's my

pre-calorie weight-loss program. First you roughhouse with your dog, then you eat a stack of pancakes. That way you don't gain weight."

"You look great the way you are." He patted my tummy.

"Are you saying I'm fat?" I teased.

"No! You're perfect! Honest!"

"All right then. Let's go eat some pancakes!"

The Jubilee was jammin' as they say in the Caribbean, not that I've ever been there. But I'm still hip. I spotted all kinds of familiar faces up early for the Pancake Breakfast. It was as if Dakota weren't dead, Miah weren't missing, and Del Ores weren't in a coma. Life went on in Frogland, no matter what, thanks to Mayor Ellington.

The mayor already held a loaded paper plate. From the line I watched him sit down at a nearby picnic table, next to a couple of promising voters who slapped his back and shook his free hand. By the time we were at the front of the pancake booth, most of the tables were full of people eating stacks.

"Yuck!" I said to the volunteer who handed me a plate.

The volunteer looked at me. "What's the matter?"

"These are green!" I hadn't noticed the unappetizing color before and made a face.

"They're Frogcakes. It's just green food coloring. Won't hurt you. Tastes the same as regular."

I looked down at the plate. The pancakes were even shaped like frogs, with a head and body and four squiggly legs.

I paid the volunteer and took my stack. While waiting for Dan to get his Frogcakes, I scanned the tables for a place to squeeze in. I found a couple of spots next to a couple more familiar faces—Janet Macavity and Simonie Scott.

"Mind if we join you?" I asked, indicating the space next to them.

"Noffallal," I think Janet said. There was some green stuff

in her mouth that obscured some of her words. I took it as a "yes" in pancake language.

"Thanks." Dan and I sat down and opened our maple syrup packets. I used the drip method of pouring, while Dan preferred the squirt method. He got to eat his pancakes sooner than I did.

After a few bites I turned to the two hospital employees and took the opportunity to ask some questions.

"Did you hear about Holly Samuels?"

The two women looked at each other, then nodded.

"How is she?"

"We can't give out that information," they both said in unison.

"Can you at least tell me if she's going to be all right?"

The women looked at each other again. Janet frowned, then said, "She's all right. She's awake and alert. Good signs. She might even be released this afternoon."

I nodded in thanks. "Good. They said she overdosed. I can hardly believe it."

Janet didn't look up from her pancakes. She just kept stabbing them and stuffing them into her mouth. Simonie grabbed her plate of half-eaten pancakes, got up from the table, and stomped away, dropping the plate into the nearest overloaded trash can. Janet watched her, chewing slowly, until Simonie disappeared into the crowd.

"Something I said?" I asked Janet.

She resumed her fast chewing, swallowed, then said, "No, she's just very upset about the death of her boyfriend, you know. Well, I better be getting back."

"You have to work today? On a Sunday?"

"No, I meant to my cooking. I'm entering one of my recipes in the Frog Cook-Off."

I blinked. The Frog Cook-Off? Did they cook with real frogs or was this just another green food coloring trick? But before I could ask her, Janet had slipped away.

"That's what I wanted to talk to you about. I think you

should enter the contest with your Hangtown Fry. After you make a small substitution," said Dan.

"You can't be serious! Put frogs in my recipe?"

"I smell chili," Dan said, sniffing the air. He put his plastic fork on his paper plate, swirled with the remaining maple syrup.

"Ugh," I said. "I'm stuffed."

"I'm still hungry. Let's head over to the Clampers' booth and see what's cooking."

"You *can't* be serious!"

But Dan was off and running. I trailed behind him as he followed the scent like a hound after a fox. When we reached the Clampers' Hellfire Chili booth, the aroma of beans, tomatoes, and chili peppers was strong enough to clear my sinuses.

"How can you eat this stuff before noon?" I asked Dan as he reached for a bowl. He dug in without answering me. "I can't watch."

I turned away—and spotted Carrie Yates, walking arm-in-arm with her husband, Burnett. They were headed my way.

I waved as the two approached. Carrie ignored me, but Burnett was polite.

"Good morning, Ms. Westphal. I believe we have an appointment later today?" Burnett said.

Dan turned around and looked at me, surprised. I ignored him.

"Actually, my uncle's had a setback. I may not be able to bring him in today. I hope that's not a problem."

"Oh, no. I understand. Whenever he's ready is fine. Just let me know."

Carrie was scanning the crowd, as if looking for someone. She still hadn't acknowledged my presence.

"Hello, Carrie," I said. "I'm glad to see you're feeling better."

She snapped her attention toward me, her face suddenly flushed. "I feel fine. What gave you the impression I wasn't?"

"I...I..." I looked at Burnett for help, but he only gave an ambiguous shake of his head. "I stopped by yesterday. Your husband said you were ill."

"Oh, I'm sick all right. Sick over the way they're treating the frogs. This kind of barbaric competition between innocent animals has got to stop."

Here we go again, I thought. Burnett suppressed an embarrassed smile, then said something to Carrie I couldn't read. She turned and began to move away. He followed, tossing me a brief apologetic glance.

"God, they're weird," I said to Dan. He was finishing up the last bite of chili. "But then, so are you. Chili for breakfast. Disgusting."

"Delicious. I'm breathing fire now."

"No kidding," I said, fanning away his peppery breath. He tried to lean in for a kiss.

I screeched and jumped away. "Get away from me, you... you dragonmouth. I'll never kiss those lips again!"

He grabbed me and planted a whopper on my mouth. Chili for breakfast wasn't so bad after all. But I'd never let him know that.

"So what now?"

"I don't know. Maybe I should sneak over to the GetWell Center while those two are here."

"But you've already been through the place a couple of times. What more do you think you'll find?"

I shrugged. "Don't know. Maybe something on Burnett. There's not much about him in the public records. He won't say where he's from."

"He's definitely a Floridian," Dan said.

I looked at him stunned. "What? How do you know?"

"The accent. Not twangy enough for Texas, not slow enough for Georgia. Gotta be Florida."

"You're kidding! You can tell where's he's from by listening to his voice?"

"Sounds just like my grandfather. He was from St. Pete. Burnett has that same soft, kinda singsongy voice."

Maybe that's why I had trouble lip-reading him, I thought. I caught a glimpse of Janet Macavity and Simonie Scott headed for the craft booths and had an idea. I turned to go.

Dan grabbed my arm. "You're not going back to GetWell, are you?"

"No," I said.

"Good. Then let's go see what else there is to eat."

"Can't," I said.

"Why not?" He raised an eyebrow.

"I've got to get to the hospital and check on Del Ores and Holly."

He raised the other eyebrow. "Connor..."

I left him holding his empty chili bowl.

Chapter 21

BUSINESS APPEARED to be slow this Sunday morning. I guess anyone who had time off was over at the Jubilee. That left a skeleton crew at Mother Lode Memorial.

Perfect.

I headed for Del Ores's room first, but wasn't allowed in by the guard-nurse. Del Rey hadn't arrived yet, but I knew she'd be there soon. I went over to Holly's room to see if I'd have better luck.

Bingo. The nurse at the station was on the phone, so I slipped into Holly's room without notice. I found her awake, staring out the window.

"Hi," I said in what I hoped was a soft voice. She gave a tenuous smile. "You're doing a whole lot better than the last time I saw you."

"I guess. I don't feel so well, though. My head is pounding."

"Are they giving you anything for it?"

"Not much. They said I need to clean out my system."

"From the gas? That seems strange."

"From the drugs."

She had taken drugs! After all her protesting, she had lied.

"Did you overdose?" I tried to say it gently but I was sure it came out harshly.

"No!" The muscles in Holly's neck tightened. "I didn't *take* any drugs!"

"But you just said…" I paused, thought a moment, and said, "Are you saying someone gave you the drugs?"

"I wouldn't have done this to myself! Not with Jonathan to look after."

"The doctor said you've been depressed."

"Yeah, sure, I've been depressed. Who isn't once in a while? But that doesn't mean I'm going to try to kill myself. I love my baby. I don't want anyone else to care for him. I miss him right now—" Tears flooded her eyes and poured down her cheeks.

I tried patting her hand but she pulled away.

"Do you know where he is?" she asked, after she'd composed herself.

"A social worker took him to a foster home. It's just temporary, until you're back on your feet."

"Unless they try to prove I tried to kill myself. Or they think I'm a druggie. I'm going to lose him, I just know it. I've seen it happen with drug moms here at the hospital all the time."

I felt helpless watching the tears stream down her face. An image of Jonathan clinging to me ran through my mind.

"I'll try to check on him. They're very secretive about that kind of information, but I'll do what I can."

Holly looked at me through reddened eyes. "Would you?"

I nodded. "Holly, you say you didn't take drugs. Then how did this happen?"

"I don't know! After work I picked up Jonathan from day care, we went over to the Jubilee for a while, stopped off at the hospital cafeteria, then we came home. I remember putting him in his crib and after that…nothing."

"How do you think you got drugged?"

"I said, I don't know! Maybe someone at the Jubilee…"

She could be right. It wouldn't have been too difficult to slip something into the food there, with the casual way it was all being served. Even someone just walking by could drop something into a drink or meal. And then there was the hospital café.

"Any idea who might want to do this to you?"

"Dakota."

"But he's dead. Anyone else?"

"I don't know. I'm too tired to think. My head is killing me."

It was time to stop the interrogation and get on with the reason I'd really come to the hospital. "Holly, one last question and then I'll leave you alone. Is there any way I can get into Janet's office or some other place that holds the hospital records?"

She shook her head. "It's almost impossible to get to the records. They're very careful with confidentiality and all that. I can't even get them without a doctor's signature. As for Janet's office, I'm sure she locks it when she's not there. Why?"

"I'm trying to find out if there's any connection between the hospital and the GetWell Center. You know, with the Medi-Cal funds or Medicare. They seem to have a rather symbiotic relationship."

"Symbi-what?"

"They seem... interdependent somehow. Any way I can find out if there's a link?"

"I'd think it would be easier to find out from GetWell than the hospital, with all our security."

"I've been to GetWell a few time. I can't find the records, but I found an interesting supply room, full of medical equipment and pharmaceuticals."

"That's hardly unusual. What about their records?"

"I guess I'll have to look again." I stood up, torn between wanting to keep my promise to leave her alone and anxious for more information. "I'll check in on you later, if that's all right."

"And my son?"

I nodded. "I'll do my best."

I headed for the door, turning to say good-bye. She said something I couldn't make out. "What?" I asked.

"I...there's one more thing."

I returned to her bedside to read her lips better.

"I've...I've been afraid to say anything. I've been getting ...notes...about Jonathan."

"Someone's been threatening you?" The hairs on my neck stood up.

"Sort of. Someone's been sending me letters saying I should keep my mouth shut."

"About Dakota?"

"No. About the hospital patients. Apparently someone overheard me when I told you about that stuff."

"What do the notes say? Do you have them?"

"I threw them away. They were too upsetting. And I wasn't exactly going to go to the sheriff. Not with what—" She stopped herself.

"Not with what, Holly? What did they say?"

"The notes said...I was going to lose Jonathan...'cause I was an unfit mother. That I took drugs and I got the drugs from the hospital." She began to weep.

"Go on. What else?"

"If I talked about what went on at the hospital, they'd make sure I lost Jonathan. They knew about my drug history—and about Dakota being my supplier."

"But who? And why? What do they want from you? I don't understand."

"I know something. About one of the patients."

"What?"

She hesitated, broke into tears again, then bit her lip in an attempt to control herself.

"One of my patients, Eugene Stadelhofer, died."

"What happened?"

"He was old, had a heart condition. Finally had a heart attack that took him. He was under my care."

"Does the hospital blame you in some way?"

She shook her head. "No, nothing like that. But...but after he died, well, I found his chart. Someone had left it behind."

"And?"

"There was no death certificate in the file."

"What did you do?"

"I set it down, meaning to report it. It was a little thing, but important for the records—and the family. But he had no family. And when I came back for the file, it was gone."

"And someone knew you'd read it."

She nodded.

"No death certificate. What does that mean?"

"If it means what I think it means..."

"Someone's still billing Medicare for his allotment."

🐾

I returned home to take Casper on a field trip. I needed some thinking time and figured there was no better place to think things through than a peaceful brook nestled among overgrown bushes.

We headed for Critter's Creek.

Casper led the way, running around like a crazed cartoon character. If I'd followed her exact path, I'd be dizzy in seconds. When we arrived at the area where Dakota had been discovered, Casper suddenly calmed down and began sniffing the ground nearby. The place was unmarked—the crime scene tape had been removed—but she knew exactly where Dakota's murder had occurred.

"What are you getting, girl?" I asked, watching her nose around the crime scene. "Smell someone familiar?" Casper barked, but I couldn't make out the dog words. Lipreading is difficult with animals. They don't have much facial expression.

I came over to Casper and gave her a pat, but she didn't calm down. She kept barking, snapping her head, and wagging her tail. Something was up. I looked around me but saw nothing out of the ordinary. I knew the Jubilee was revving up, and wondered if Casper was barking at the distant noise.

Suddenly she stopped barking and began licking the water.

"No!" I shouted, and gave the sign for "no" at the same time. She stopped drinking and sat down. I pulled out a plastic bowl from my backpack, filled it with water from a bottle I'd brought, and gave it to her to drink. She lapped it up with vigor.

"Good girl." I patted her as she drank. When she finished, she sat down, drooled a bit, then lay down on her tummy and rested. I squatted down next to her, staring into the creek water, trying to imagine Dakota at the scene.

What was he doing there? Trying to poison the frogs? Getting rid of drug evidence? Something else?

Suddenly Casper stood up at full alert, then sprinted wildly into the bushes, after a rabbit, no doubt. I watched her run, knowing she'd come back eventually, but called her anyway. This wasn't exactly the safest neighborhood, for animals or humans. That thought gave me a sudden shudder. It probably wasn't the best place for me—

I didn't have time to finish my thought. Someone shoved me violently from behind. I fell into the creek, face first, the wind knocked out of my chest. I lifted my head, gasping for breath, getting nothing.

Sputtering, I tried to get up on my hands and knees, but the attacker pushed me down into the water, then pressed his foot on my back. I swished my head back and forth, trying to break free, taking in gulps of creek water each time I tried to breathe.

The more I tried to push up, the heavier the weight came down on my back. Helpless, I splashed around, and tried to roll out from under him. But he had the advantage, with his foot on my back. All I could do was flounder in the water— and attempt to grab a breath of air.

I tried again to move out from under the pressure, but as I nearly wriggled free, the full weight of the attacker's body came slamming down on top of me.

I was underwater. Unable to move. Unable to breathe. Unable to think.

I grabbed behind my back, but couldn't reach anything. Straining to open my eyes, I saw nothing but murky brown water. The attacker held my hair, forcing my face straight down into the creek bed. My lungs began to burn.

I needed air. I needed it so badly, I nearly took a breath underwater. Just as I started to see splotches, I felt a release.

With every last bit of strength I had left, I shoved myself up, out of the water, and gasped. A full breath of air filled my lungs. I hung my head, still on my hands and knees, and just breathed. I breathed until my lungs stopped burning and my head was spinning from too much oxygen. Dizzy, I pushed myself to a sitting position and wiped my wet, stringy hair back over my forehead. It was several more seconds before my vision cleared.

When I looked around, I didn't see my attacker. Instead, I saw the most beautiful thing I'd ever seen in my life.

Casper.

She was soaking wet and barking her head off. I reached out for her, and she stepped into the creek with me. Wrapping my arms around her, I hugged her until she wriggled free. I looked down at her and saw the blood. One of her toenails had been ripped off.

She had scared off my attacker and had lost a toenail in the battle.

What a dog.

"Casper!" I said, rubbing her fur, probably too hard to feel good to her. "You're my hero!"

She licked my face—mud, creek water, and all—and didn't seem to mind the disgusting taste. "Let's get you to the vet," I said, pulling myself up slowly. Muscles ached where I didn't know I had muscles. I bent down to retrieve my backpack and noticed something I was certain hadn't been there before.

A small pill bottle with the label ripped off.

It was empty.

Chapter 22

I PICKED UP the pill bottle and examined it. Stupid, I know. There might have been fingerprints on it. Blame it on a lack of oxygen. Anyway, the bottle was clearly empty. Did that mean it had been full a short time ago? If so, what was inside? I clutched my stomach. And where was it now?

I burped up a mouthful of creek water and spat it out, wondering if it was poisoned with something from the bottle. Either way, it tasted foul. I had a feeling there was more where that came from. Maybe after I took Casper to the vet, I'd have my stomach pumped. Or not.

I sat in the vet's office waiting for the doctor to tell me if Casper would ever play the violin again. When I wasn't thinking about Casper and all the good times we'd had over the years, I thought about the creek and Dakota and my attacker.

The attack on me made me question everything I'd been thinking about Dakota. What if he hadn't been trying to poison the water? What if he was, say, collecting samples of the water to have it analyzed—and someone tried to stop him. And succeeded. The same person who attacked me?

So maybe he was killed because he knew something about the creek water. And maybe the same person tried to kill me because he or she thought I knew something about the water. But what?

At that point my imagination went kind of crazy. I started dreaming up all kinds of scenarios involving Dakota. It was probably the stomach full of creek water talking, but I began to wonder if maybe someone drugged him first, like they did Holly, then shoved him under the water to drown him. The toxicology report wasn't in yet, but I had a hunch Arthurlene would find something in his blood that didn't belong.

If he were drugged, he'd have been easier to drown. Dakota was a strong guy. It would take a lot to hold him down, unless he'd been sedated in some way first. Then again, he could have been under the influence, of his own accord. After all, he was a drug dealer. And dealers often did their own stuff.

But what about Miah? What did he have to do with any of this? And where the hell was he?

After half an hour, the vet came out of the surgery and announced that Casper would be fine, but she wanted to keep her overnight for observation. Just like a real hospital. I gave her a last pat good-bye, but she didn't respond, still under the anesthetic. I checked her foot. Where one of her toenails should have been, there was a thick white bandage.

Poor thing.

When I got ahold of whoever did this, I was going to rip their toenails off.

I stopped by the sheriff's office to report my creek encounter, but the dispatcher, Rebecca Matthews, said he was out. No matter what's going on in Flat Skunk or my personal life, Rebecca always puts a smile on my face, just for being who she is. Today the octogenarian wore a muumuu, combat boots, and about two dozen butterfly clips in her orange-gray hair. She was working on a scrapbook of the Backstreet Boys at her desk. I decided not to ask.

I thought about telling Dan, then decided I didn't want the hassle of him telling me I should mind my own business so things like this wouldn't happen to me. Screw that. I headed for the hospital.

"You smell like pond scum," Del Rey said, wrinkling up her nose as I entered Del Ores's room.

"Thank you. It's a new perfume I got on sale. It's called Swamp Water. Bought a vat of it for a dollar ninety-nine. Got you some, too."

Del Rey smiled, but her heart wasn't in it. As she sat by Del Ores's bedside, her tired eyes told the real story.

"Getting any sleep?" I asked, pulling up a chair.

She shrugged. "Not as much as Del Ores."

"Any change?"

"Nothing much. I can see her eyes rolling under the lids. And she moves her mouth now and then, but that's it. Maybe you can lip-read her. She doesn't say anything loud enough for me to actually hear."

I gave Del Rey a pat on the hand.

"So how'd you get in here, anyway?" Del Rey asked. "It's supposed to be family only and one person at a time. You're breaking two rules."

"I learned a long time ago that if you act like you belong somewhere, people don't notice that you don't. Being deaf, it's especially easy. We're always overlooked. Kind of like being invisible."

Del Rey laughed. "You sneaked in, didn't you?"

I made a face.

Out of the corner of my eye, I saw Del Ores twitch.

"Did you see that?" I asked Del Rey.

She nodded. "Happens a lot. Involuntary reflex or spasm of some kind. Don't get your hopes—"

Del Ores opened her eyes.

"Oh my God, she's awake!" Del Rey said, pushing the button for the nurse.

"Welcome back," I said to Del Ores, leaning over her. Her blind gaze flitted around. She tried to say something but I couldn't make out her words.

The nurse appeared immediately and began checking Del Ores's blood pressure and IV. We backed up to give her room to work. Del Ores's gaze continued to flit wildly around the room.

"She's stable. I'll get the doctor," the nurse said, then rushed out of the room.

Del Ores lifted her head as if listening for some specific sound. Del Rey moved closer and held her sister's hand. Del Ores said something but Del Rey didn't seem to understand. I moved in closer, but still couldn't read the lips that barely moved. Del Ores tried to speak again. I watched her lips closely, trying to make out the words. Then I looked at Del Rey.

"What's she saying?" Del Rey leaned forward, hope shining on her face.

"I...I can't make it out...." I watched Del Ores's lips intently. "Oh, my God...that can't be right...."

Del Rey jiggled my elbow. "What? What's she saying?"

"I can't be sure...but it looked like, 'You smell like chili.'"

Del Rey stared at me in disbelief. "Chili! You can't be serious. First of all, you smell like pond scum. And second of all, the first words my sister says when she comes out of a coma are not likely to be, 'You smell like chili.'"

Del Ores was still moving her lips. She coughed, swallowed, then moved her lips again.

Del Rey clutched my arm.

"My God, you were right!" Del Rey said, grinning through tears. "I could hear her that time. She said, 'You smell like chili.'"

Pond scum I could understand. But chili?

Del Rey and I were asked to leave the room when the doctor appeared, moments later. After half an hour of anxious waiting, they allowed us back in. Del Ores, still conscious, grinned when she heard us enter. She was going to be all right.

"Thank God!" were Del Rey's first words when she saw her sister again.

Mine were: "Do you want some chili?" I'd heard about coma patients waking up and craving some particular food.

Del Ores shook her head, then reached out in my direction. I moved closer and she took me by the shoulders. Pulling me down toward her, she tucked her nose in my hair—and inhaled deeply.

I read her lips when she let go. "You smell like chili."

Del Rey and I laughed. We'd never forget those first words.

"Thanks, Del Ores. Your sister thinks I smell like pond scum. I prefer your olfactory perception."

"Oh, you do smell like pond scum," Del Ores added quickly. "On your skin. And your breath smells like...blueberry?"

My mouth dropped open. "I...I had blueberry pancakes for breakfast. Wow, you're good. But I didn't have any chili. Except a taste." I blushed, thinking about Dan's kiss.

"No, it's not your breath. It's your hair. Definitely a hint of chili powder."

I tried to pull a strand over to my nose but it wouldn't reach. "I thought I was good at deciphering body language, and I'm pretty good with smells, too. But you've really got a gift."

"She's amazing," Del Rey said. "One time I took a cookie from my mother's freshly baked supply, then rearranged all the cookies so you couldn't tell one was missing. Del Ores knew the moment she entered my bedroom, just by the smell!"

"Do all blind people have enhanced smelling ability?" I asked, then regretted it. It was similar to a question I received from hearing people: "Do all deaf people have enhanced vision?"

Del Ores smiled. Apparently she'd heard the question before, too, much as I had with my own disability. "No, we don't have Superman's ability to smell speeding bullets or anything. But when you lose one sense, you tend to concentrate more on the ones remaining. And there's some research now that indicates some brain cells grow larger in certain areas, depending on how much another sense is used."

"Really? I thought it was all just an old wives' tale. That we really didn't have any more capacity than those with all five senses. So you're saying, our brains kind of make up for the lack of one sense, by expanding the area for the other senses. Makes sense, so to speak."

"I'm extremely sensitive to smells. To a fault. It sometimes distracts me, when I can't get past a smell. Like the chili."

"Yes, but...I think you're wrong on that one. Like I said—"

"Bizarre, I know, but that's my take on it." Del Ores was slowing down. Her initial energy seemed to be depleting quickly. It would be moments before we were hustled out again, to let Del Ores get her rest. Not that she needed a nap.

Sure enough, the nurse entered the room. We stood, gave Del Ores a hug, and told her we'd be back soon.

"Thank God," Del Rey said, on the way back to the waiting room. "She's going to be all right."

"I knew she would be. She's from hearty stock. Except... what do you make of that chili smell? Some kind of post-coma olfactory sensation?"

Del Rey leaned in and smelled my hair.

"You know, once you get past the pond scum, you do smell like chili."

So where did I get the chili-smelling hair?

I felt again the horror of someone holding me under the creek water.

Whoever it was had reeked of chili—and had been holding me by my hair.

Chapter 23

CHILI IN MY HAIR. There was only one way that could have happened: the person who grabbed my hair and forced me into the water must have had chili powder on his or her hands.

The Calaveras Chili Cook-Off!

I checked my watch. The event was due to take place at 1:00 P.M. Had my attacker been practicing culinary skills along with killing skills? It was very possible he—or she—would be at the Cook-Off in some capacity.

I had to be there. It wouldn't be enough to sit in the audience and try to guess who was riddled with chili powder. I needed to be on the stage to let the attacker know I wasn't threatened.

And, with the help of Dan, I had a plan to get him to reveal himself.

I headed for the Chili Cook-Off tent, where the chefs were probably sautéing, boiling, frying, or doing whatever it was they did to their chili recipes to make them winners.

As I expected, Dan was hovering over a big pot, adding chili powder and stirring a thick red mass of tomatoes, beans, meat, and spices. The tent reeked of chili powder, garlic, onions, and more chili powder. The smell cleared my sinuses instantly.

"Dan!"

He jumped. Chili powder flew. Wasn't expecting me, I guess.

"Jesus, Connor! What are you trying to do? Scare the chef?"

"Sorry. Don't know my own voice level sometimes. You know how it is."

He gave a half grin. "What's up?" He returned to his stirring. I liked the domestic look it gave him. Especially the checkered apron that read DON'T **** WITH THE COOK.

"I...need a favor."

"Uh-oh."

"I need to enter a recipe in the Chili Cook-Off."

"Too late. You had to have your entry in last week."

"I know."

It took him a moment.

"No way. I was only kidding when I said you should enter something. I'm worried about you, and I don't want you getting so involved."

"Dan, please! I need to do this. I was—" I hesitated. He could be so overprotective. "I went to the creek to look over the site again...and...someone grabbed me. But I got away."

"What?" Dan stood there with his mouth open, and his spoon raised.

"Everything's all right. Really. But the one who attacked me, he...he smelled like chili."

"Him and several thousand other people here. Not much of a clue, Connor."

"It wasn't his breath. It was his hands."

"He had his hands on you?"

"In my hair."

Dan leaned forward and sniffed. "I don't smell anything."

"You can't smell anything in here but chili!"

He shrugged.

"Dan?"

"Connor! I worked hard on this recipe. It's my dad's 'Whup-Ass Chili.' He used to make it every year at the Policeman's Roundup. This is killer."

"Not a very good term to use at the moment, do you think?"

He turned back to his pot and stirred a little more vigorously than he needed to. After a few moments, he turned back.

"What do you plan to do?"

"I thought I'd tell the judges you were sick and that I was entering the chili for you. Then when it comes time for the tasting, I've got a plan that should rattle the snake who attacked me. I think it's the same person who killed Dakota."

"This is ridiculous."

"Maybe. But worth a try. Can I have a taste?" I took the wooden spoon from him and nibbled a bit from the end.

I couldn't talk for about five minutes afterward.

The audience that filled the grandstand for the Cook-Off was considerably smaller than last year's. Probably due to the death of Dakota. Sometimes a sensational crime will bring in the ambulance-chasers, but this time it seemed that fewer people stayed to see if someone else might also bite the dust. Death was entertainment these days, when it didn't involve personal risk to the onlooker.

I made a quick trip to one of the many Jubilee kiosks to pick up a few souvenirs, then joined the contestants who were headed for the stage. They all carried their pots and vats of homemade secret-recipe chili and placed them on their marked spots for the judges to taste. I recognized several people in the competition, including Mayor Ellington in his frog outfit, Janet Macavity, overdressed for the occasion and the weather in long sleeves and pants, Simonie Scott, practically Janet's opposite in a too-short skirt and too-low-cut top, and Burnett Pike, looking haggard and worn. The only one I didn't expect was Carrie Yates.

"Hi Carrie," I said, as she set her pot down next to mine. I felt in my pocket for my souvenirs.

"Ms. Westphal," she said without smiling. She turned to her husband standing next to her, his own bowl of chili in front of him. Carrie seemed fine, not at all the unstable woman I'd seen in the sheriff's office, or the sick woman that Burnett had described.

I tapped her on the shoulder. "Vegetarian?" I asked, indicating her entry.

"Of course," she said proudly.

Mayor Ellington stood on my other side, too busy waving to the crowd to comment on my appearance in the contest. Simonie stood next to him, with Janet beside her.

The judges formed a line at one end of the table while the contest rules were announced. I couldn't hear them, but I saw the MC's lips flapping and figured he wasn't saying anything too important. I checked the stands for Dan, and found him hiding under a large cowboy hat, trying to be inconspicuous, seeing as how he was supposed to be sick. I signed, "Thanks," and he nodded.

I hoped he hadn't forgotten what he was supposed to do.

As the judges began moving down the table, lifting lids off the chili pots and dunking their spoons into the spicy concoctions, somebody threw a rubber frog at one of the judges, and the woman let out a scream.

At least I assume she screamed. Everyone looked in the direction of the outburst. Everyone except me.

While the contestants had their heads turned toward the excitement, I quickly moved down the line, lifting pot lids and dropping in the contents of my pocket.

After the startled judge quieted down and resumed her chili tasting, I nodded another "thanks" to Dan. He'd done well—and his aim had been perfect. The judges continued down the row, tasting each entry with poker faces. Carrie's was next. The three judges crowded around her pot, raised their clean spoons, and waited for Carrie to lift the lid. As soon as she did, two chili-covered windup frogs hopped out.

One judge screamed as a frog, dripping with chili, hit her

face. Another judge nearly toppled off the stage. The third just looked disgusted. When the rest of the contestants realized what had happened, they all lifted the lids on their chili pots.

Windup frogs went flying all over the place.

In the meantime, Carrie had lost all her color.

"What's the meaning of this?" said the disgusted judge.

Carrie could only stammer. She looked out at the crowd laughing at the spectacle. Her lips were tight, her eyebrows clenched, her face grew ugly. She whirled around to me, eyes wide with hatred, and screamed, "You put those frogs in my chili!"

I stepped back to avoid the spittle coming at me, but the stage was crowded with judges, contestants, and pots of hot chili. Suddenly Carrie lunged for me.

"You're trying to make a fool out of me! You're trying to discredit all the work I've done for LEAP! How dare you!"

I don't know where the knife came from, but Carrie held it above her head, ready to strike.

All hell broke loose. Contestants and judges leapt from the stage, while a few men close by tried to get up on the stage and stop the maniacal woman. While dodging the slashes with the knife, I didn't see Dan at first as he hoisted himself up onto the stage. He had joined Burnett in trying to subdue Carrie and keep her from carving me up into chili ingredients.

She got in one last lunge before they stopped her. I felt the knife slice my arm.

"She cut me!" I yelled, as Dan and Burnett took control of Carrie. Burnett held onto her while Dan grabbed my arm and wrapped it with a nearby chef's towel. In the corner of my eye, I could see Carrie writhing and screaming, but my attention was locked on my arm.

In a matter of moments, Sheriff Mercer arrived.

"What the hell happened here?" he asked, glancing at my arm, then at Carrie, then back at me.

"She...cut me. She just flipped out!"

Dan said nothing. But I knew what he was thinking—that

I had baited her, along with everyone else. I had teased a mental case and she had lost it. It was my fault, and I was trying to shift the blame to Carrie.

The sheriff went over to talk with Burnett and get his side of the story. All I could see was head-shaking, as if he didn't have a clue what had caused her to react so violently.

I guess she thought the frogs were real.

Dan looked at me long and hard.

"What?"

He continued to stare at me.

"I just thought..."

"You just thought if you put some fake frogs in her chili, she'd try to attack you, like you think she did at the creek. Pretty stupid, Connor. She could have killed you."

I looked down at my throbbing arm. It hurt like hell. And so did my conscience.

I watched as Burnett gave Carrie some pills to take, then led her away. She slumped against him, as if all the energy had drained from her body. I noticed Simonie Scott watching Carrie and wondered what she was thinking.

Sheriff Mercer returned to fill us in. "Burnett says she's been under a lot of strain recently. Really upset about all this frog business. Taking it too seriously, I guess."

"Sheriff, do you think she's capable of murder?" I asked. I briefly filled him in on my creek experience.

He paused a moment. "I haven't ruled her out. She's strong as a horse. She had plenty of opportunity. And she has access to drugs, which she could have used to sedate him before drowning him."

"What's her motive?" I asked. "Some kind of drug thing?" I told the sheriff what I knew about Dakota's access to drugs and his dealings. "But how does that tie into Carrie Yates?"

The sheriff said nothing. But I had a gnawing feeling he considered her the primary suspect. After all, she had tried to kill me.

Chapter 24

I SPENT THE AFTERNOON at my office, worrying about Miah, wondering about Carrie, and watching for my TTY to ring with information on the whereabouts of Holly's son, Jonathan. Too distracted to get much work done, I finally headed for the hospital to join Del Rey and Del Ores for dinner. Del Ores would be having the Jell-O Supreme. Del Rey and I were bringing our own deli sandwiches.

When I arrived at Mother Lode Memorial, I was surprised to find Sheriff Mercer in the lobby.

"Sheriff!" I cut him off as he was about to head out.

"Hey, C.W., what are you doing here? Come to put frogs in the patients' food?"

"Sheriff! It was a harmless little prank. I had no idea she'd turn so violent."

"Yeah, well, now you know. So stay away from her. She'll be here overnight for observation, then we'll talk about whether or not you want to press charges for the assault."

I held up my hands. "No, no! I don't want to press charges. How is she?"

"Dazed. Confused. They've sedated her, so she hasn't said much. Just keeps repeating frog-related gibberish over and over. Makes no sense to me. Not to Burnett either."

"He's there with her?"

"Yep. Said she's been taking lithium to help her mood swings. But she quit taking her meds a few days ago and hasn't been herself. He's real worried about her."

"She's been on prescription antidepressants?" I asked.

"Not an authorized prescription, apparently. Burnett says she's been treating herself, ever since her first husband died."

I thought about the closet at the GetWell Center, filled with medical equipment and pharmaceuticals. "I suppose she's been getting the drugs from her own supply room."

Sheriff Mercer shook his head. "Burnett swears she hasn't gone in there. He and the charge nurse are the only ones with the keys, and she's not allowed to have them. Burnett said she overdosed awhile back and that scared him. Took away her key and thought that would be the end of it."

"And it wasn't?"

"Apparently not."

"You mean, she's been getting the drugs from someone else?"

"That's what Burnett seems to think."

"Does he know who from?"

The sheriff said nothing and glanced toward the door.

"Sheriff? What are you holding back?"

Sheriff Mercer licked his lips, then faced me. "I'm going to have to arrest Carrie once she's well enough to leave the hospital, C.W."

"Why, because she's been medicating herself? Or because she tried to...attack me—"

"I'm officially charging her with the murder of Dakota Webster."

Del Rey burst into the lobby, carrying a bag of what I imagined were sandwiches, grinning like a sister who's just found her long-lost twin.

"There you are! Sorry I'm late. I was..." She looked at both of us and the smile disappeared. "What's wrong? Has something happened to Del Ores? I can see it in your faces. Tell me!"

"Calm down, Del Rey," Sheriff Mercer said. "I'm sure your sister is fine. We were discussing something else."

I turned back to the sheriff. "Yeah, you want to explain what you just said? About arresting Carrie for Dakota's murder?"

"What, you think Miah's a more likely suspect?"

"Of course not. But Carrie? She can hardly hold her head up."

"Except when she's got a knife in her hand."

He had me there. "What grounds do you have to arrest her?"

"Burnett said something after Carrie was given her sedative."

"What?"

"Look, I can't say anything right now. I gotta go get a warrant to search her place, not to mention an arrest warrant. Don't say anything about this. Burnett would like to keep it as quiet as possible until—"

"He says his wife murdered Dakota Webster—and he wants to keep it quiet? Not likely in this community. What did he say, exactly?"

Sheriff Mercer sighed. "He said, Dakota's been supplying Carrie with lithium for the past six months. A week ago he threatened to cut off her supply. So she started following him around. She said she put something in his bottled water over at the Jubilee while he was working with his frog. He went down to the creek for some reason, maybe to find more frogs, and that's when he drank the water. When he started acting woozy, she pushed him into the water and sat on him until he drowned."

Just like she tried to do to me. I shivered.

"But...but..." I had nothing to go with the buts. It all made sense. I just didn't want it to. Not that I wanted Miah to be a suspect. But Carrie? A murderer?

And then her lunge with the knife flashed back to mind and my arm ached with the memory. Someone once said anyone is capable of murder given the right circumstances. I think it was one of the Three Stooges.

"So you're really going to arrest Carrie for the murder of Dakota?"

"As soon as I finish searching her place. Burnett said we'd find the evidence in her bedroom."

"Burnett's being awfully cooperative, isn't he?"

"He's very concerned about her, C.W. He's hoping she'll get diminished capacity and be sent to a mental hospital, not prison. He's going to do all he can to help her. The guy's crazy about her. After all, he's been protecting her all this time, when he knew everything."

I nodded. The sheriff gave a two-fingered salute and moved on out the exit, leaving Del Rey and me in stunned silence.

After a few moments, Del Rey raised the paper bag and awoke me from my daydream.

"Shall we?" she said. I nodded, and followed her to Del Ores's room, where we were met by another surprise.

"Del Ores! What are you doing up? And dressed?"

Del Ores turned in our direction and grinned. A nurse stood next to her, helping her load her things into a plastic hospital bag.

"The doctor said I could go home. I just need to take it easy."

Del Rey rushed to hug Del Ores, the sandwich bag still in her hands. Del Ores sniffed the air. "Is that roast beef I smell? You better have enough for me. I'm through with tapioca pudding."

"I've got a better idea!" I announced. "Let's go to my diner, I'll whip up some Hangtown Fry, Connor-style, and we'll celebrate. How does that sound?"

"That's very sweet of you, Connor," Del Ores said, reaching out for my hand. "I don't want you to go to any trouble."

"The way I cook, it's never trouble. And sometimes it's edible."

The sisters laughed. We finished packing up Del Ores, and Del Rey led her down the hall, with me in the rear.

When we arrived at my diner, the first thing I noticed was the lack of a wet and sloppy greeting by Casper. She was still at the vet, and the place seemed especially lonely without her.

I was glad I'd invited the sisters over for dinner. I needed the company as much as they needed the celebration.

Del Rey led Del Ores around my living area, explaining all my gadgets for the deaf. She gently touched my TTY machine, my closed caption box attached to my old TV, my Shake-Awake alarm, and my phone light. Watching her examine each item as if her fingers could see was a beautiful sight—one that Del Ores would never enjoy the way I could. But then, she had music and birdsong and all those other wonderful sounds that hearing people are always talking about.

Del Rey and Del Ores sat at the table as I brought on my version of Hangtown Fry. I joined them, then watched Del Ores as she positioned her food. Del Rey told her where the items on her plate were located, using a clock face as a guide.

"The pasta is at ten o'clock, the salad at six, the bread at two. Salt and pepper are to your right, and the soda is to your left. Try not to spill it."

I shot Del Rey a look, surprised at the rudeness of her comment. But Del Ores laughed.

"It's a running joke," Del Rey said. "I'm always kidding her about spilling stuff."

"Occupational hazard with me," Del Ores added, as she slowly moved her hands forward. "When I was a kid, I tended to wear more of my food than eat it." She located her glass of soda and the condiments, then felt for her fork. Oriented to her plate, she dug into the pasta at ten o'clock. Only once did she lift an empty fork.

Del Ores and I chatted throughout dinner, comparing notes on how we were treated with our disabilities. I told her how hearing people always overemphasize their words when they find out I lip-read, which only makes them harder to understand. She shared stories about sighted people who tried to help her across the street by grabbing her arm and forcing her.

"It's so simple, but sighted people don't think about it," Del

Rey added. "All you have to do is let the blind person take your elbow, and then just lead them across the street. They need to feel they're in control."

"I really don't need anyone to help me much," Del Ores continued. "We're trained in mobility and orientation at school. We've learned how to position ourselves in space, walk with a cane, listen for traffic, beware of obstacles, that kind of thing. We're much more independent than people think."

I watched her reach for her soda. She picked up the glass and knew by the weight it was empty. I started to reach for the soda bottle, but Del Rey waved my hand away. Del Ores moved her hand slowly, searching for the bottle, and found it in seconds. I wondered if she'd listened to where I had placed it earlier. She pulled the glass toward her, then put her finger just over the side of the rim. Slowly, expertly, she poured the soda into her glass until the liquid touched her finger. Setting the bottle down where it had been originally, she licked her soda-dipped finger, then took a sip.

"And for my next performance..." Del Ores said with a grin.

"Sorry," I said, feeling myself blush. "I'm just fascinated."

"Well, that TTY is quite a gadget, where you type your conversation back and forth instead of saying it out loud. And your Shake-Awake alarm! How cool."

We cleaned up the dishes and headed for the living area. I thought about suggesting a video, then realized Del Ores wouldn't be able to see it and kicked myself mentally.

"I'm bushed," Del Rey said. I was lucky to be able to read her lips through the yawn. "It's been a helluva day. We should get going."

"Uh-oh," Del Ores said suddenly, feeling her coat. "I've lost my wallet! It must have fallen out when I was leaving the hospital."

"Oh no. Can it wait until tomorrow?" Del Rey said, checking her watch.

"I suppose, but I hate the idea of my wallet lying around somewhere there. Can't we run back and get it?"

"You need to get your rest, Del Ores," Del Rey said. "Tell you what. I'll drive you home, then go back to the hospital and see if I can find your wallet."

"I've got a better idea," I said. "I'll drive Del Ores home so you can go directly to the hospital for the wallet. That way you don't have to double back, and it's no big deal for me to drive her to your place."

We agreed it was the best solution. Del Rey gave me a hug and headed out the door to her car.

"Give me one minute to find my keys," I said to Del Ores. She stood patiently waiting in the hallway.

"Take your time. In fact, I'm going to use your bathroom really quick before we go."

I found my keys, waited for Del Ores, then led her toward the passenger side of my Chevy, nearly tripping on a loose twig. Del Rey had already gone by the time we got outside. "God, it's dark out here," I said. "I can't see a thing."

I regretted the words as soon as they came out, and I realized how hearing people must feel when they use the words "hear" and "sound" around me. If Del Ores was like me, she was used to these faux pas. Either she said nothing or it was too dark to read her lips. As we reached the car, she let go of my arm and opened the door. The inside light lit her face dimly.

"Do you want me to drive?" she asked. I was taken aback for a moment, then realized she was making a joke and laughed.

"Maybe next time," I said, and moved around to the driver's side. I slid in, pulled the car door closed, and fastened my seat belt. Del Ores's belt was already locked.

I thought Del Ores said something, but I couldn't read her in the dark with the inside light off. I flicked it on and asked her to repeat while I watched her lips.

"I said, 'Chicken.'"

I laughed and stuck the key in the ignition, shifted gears, adjusted the rearview mirror, and started to let off the parking brake, when someone reared up behind me and grabbed me around the neck.

Suddenly I couldn't breathe.

Chapter 25

I TRIED TO COUGH OUT, "Del Ores" to alert her, but I could hardly take in air, let alone speak. If Del Ores knew what was going on, I had no way of knowing. All I could do was fight to keep the attacker from strangling me.

I grabbed at my neck and tried to loosen whatever it was that cut off my air, but I couldn't get a grip. My vision was starting to go and my head throbbed. I had a sense that Del Ores was touching my leg, but I was too frantic trying to breathe to really know.

With one hand still on the garrote, I swung my other hand back over my head and tried to connect with the attacker. I ended up hurting my wrist as it slammed against the attacker's head. Apparently the blow had no impact. The noose tightened. My head felt as if it would burst. My fingers were numb and cold.

"Del Ores," I mouthed. No response. Finally, I grabbed her arm and pulled it toward me to show her what was happening. I felt her arm tense and taut, her body rigid. She knew something was going on.

I felt something in her hand. Hard, stiff, cold.

It whipped past my face, just brushing my cheek.

And then the choke hold loosened.

I pulled at the rope that had been cutting off my airway and took some short gasps of air. Then I spun around and saw Del Ores, her cane folded in half, whacking madly at someone in the backseat.

My attacker, wearing a mask that looked like a frog, with the eyes and mouth cut out, was being caned senseless by a blind woman!

After two more whacks, the intruder shoved open the back door to the Chevy and rolled out. Del Ores kept hitting the backseat unaware that the attacker had escaped. I let her keep going for a few moments, while I leaned over and locked all four car doors, narrowly missing a whack in the process. I managed to say, "Stop! He's gone." She hit the backseat two more times with lessening intensity, then sank into her seat, breathless, her cane across her lap.

"He's gone, he's gone," I rasped, like a mantra. "I locked the doors. We're safe." I took a few more aching breaths, then held Del Ores's hand. "God, you're quite a caner! You...saved my life, that's for sure."

Del Ores caught her breath, then spoke. "Where did he come from? All of a sudden I felt you stiffen and I could hear you gasping. At first I thought you were having a heart attack or something. Then I heard someone behind you, breathing heavily, grunting. All I could do was try to scare him off with my cane."

"Well, you did just that. And you invented a new form of self-defense. But he could still be out there somewhere. We've got to get the sheriff."

I reached for my keys in the ignition—and felt the empty space where the keys had been.

"My keys!" In a panic, I felt around the floor for them. I never had a chance to find them. The back window of my Chevy imploded, sending glass shards showering around my head. I screamed. I'm sure Del Ores did, too. Glancing in my rearview mirror, petrified with fear, I saw the masked attacker trying to climb in.

He had dropped the hammer, and held a bottle of something in his hand.

"Get out of the car!" I shouted to Del Ores. I knew the attacker was after me. I grabbed the door handle and pulled.

Locked!

I pulled at the button lock, missing three times, as I shoved my shoulder against the door. It finally opened and I fell out onto the driveway, landing on my side. The gravel bit into my hip and shoulder, tearing my shirt and pants.

I scrambled up, skin burning, and tried to run for the diner. I took only a step before the wind was knocked out of me by the tackling assailant as I hit the ground again, the air forced from my lungs. I scraped my jaw against the gravel and felt my lip split. Blood dripped onto the driveway.

I tried to get up on my hands and knees, but the attacker landed on my back and knocked me flat. Before I could move, he rolled me over and started hitting me in the stomach and face. I tried lifting my head but he slammed it down and I nearly blacked out.

Woozy, I tried to open my eyes. My arms and legs were pinned down by my attacker's body and knees. Unable to move, all I could do was watch through blurred vision as he raised an arm over my head. In his hand he held the same small bottle I'd seen in the car. I couldn't read the label, but I made out the poison symbol in the dim porch light.

The attacker grinned through the mouth hole of the frog mask, his outlined lips enhanced and clearly readable.

"What's the worst thing that could happen to a deaf person?"

I spit at him in response.

He shook off the saliva, then said, "I'll bet it's going blind."

Raising the bottle in his hand, he twisted off the cap with the other.

I had a good idea what was inside.

Acid.

Suddenly the bottle jerked up, and the burning liquid splashed out, missing my face by inches. I felt a few drops singe my ear, but was too focused on getting away from the attacker, now that he'd let go of his vise grip.

It was his voice that had given away his location. Not to me, but to Del Ores, who stood over him, thrashing him, not with her thin metal cane, but with a tire iron she must have pulled from the trunk of my Chevy.

That poor, helpless blind woman was one strong, clever adversary, at least with adrenaline added to the insulin.

I actually had to stop Del Ores from beating to death the crumpled figure on the ground.

"He's down, Del Ores. For good, this time." I touched her arm that held the weapon.

She wheezed, still clutching the tire iron.

"How'd you find it?" I asked, gently taking it from her.

"Got your keys," she puffed, "from the floor where you dropped them. Opened the trunk. Knew there must be one in there. Del Rey has one in her car, and she had to use it one day to fix a flat tire. Felt around until I found it." She panted some more.

"How'd you locate the attacker?"

"Heard you scuffling. I just listened until I was pretty sure of the location. Then when she starting talking, I knew exactly where to aim."

"She?" I said, looking down at the barely breathing body by my feet.

I pulled off the mask.

I could just make out the identity of the bloodied and swollen face.

Janet Macavity, Mother Lode Hospital's business manager.

Chapter 26

JANET LAY UNCONSCIOUS, too battered to need restraining, but we decided not to take any chances. I ran in and dialed the sheriff on the TTY, and managed to catch him in the office.

"YEah CW what is itt? GA" he typed in his familiar, garbled way.

I quickly typed in the scenario, making plenty of mistakes myself. "Hurry!! SK SK" I signed off, then returned to help Del Ores, who had managed to tie up Janet with the rope I'd found in my Chevy—the rope Janet had used to try to strangle me. Del Ores used her cane as a brace across the woman's back. It seemed fitting.

We sat outside waiting for the sheriff. When Janet regained consciousness, we tried to get her to talk, but she mostly drooled or spat blood. By the time he arrived, she was coherent and beginning to fight her restraints.

Sheriff Mercer jumped out of his car the moment he drove up, leaving the car door open in his haste.

"What the hell—" He turned away and I missed the rest of his question. Del Ores must have heard him clearly, though. She began telling the story from her side. I just watched her lips to make sure she covered everything. She only left out the part about the acid, which I had washed off before phoning the sheriff. I had to add that. It had made a big impression on me.

Janet remained mute. She refused to talk without her attorney present, and Sheriff Mercer didn't push it. Me, I was dying to find out why the hell she tried to kill me—twice—and why she probably murdered Dakota. For the present, I could only imagine various scenarios.

"Del Ores, C.W., you two need to go to the hospital and get checked out," Sheriff Mercer said, after loading a handcuffed Janet Macavity into the backseat of his patrol car. "You both look like you lost your WWF fights. You need a ride?" The sheriff handed over Del Ores's cane, which she folded into four neat sections. It was now small enough to fit inside her pocket again.

I offered to drive, then felt the sting in my knees where the gravel was embedded, and the burning on my ear where the acid had made contact and changed my mind.

"I guess we do." I hobbled into the front seat next to Del Ores. Turning to the backseat, I made sure the safety glass between the front and back was attack-proof. I didn't want any more surprise garrotings on the way to the hospital.

"Sheriff, would you call my sister and let her know where I'm going?" Del Ores asked. "I was supposed to be there some time ago. I'm sure she's worried."

"She's got good reason, don't you think?" the sheriff said. He got on his radio and made the call, which I couldn't hear. Good thing. I'll bet Del Rey was yelling loud enough to further deafen the already hard-of-hearing sheriff.

An hour later Del Ores and I were patched up, and we both had escorts home. Dan had arrived to offer his support and I-told-you-so's, while Del Rey came to comfort her sister. I wished I had a sister at that moment, with Dan blubbering about how glad he was that I was alive, then blabbering about how I'm always getting into trouble and why can't I just be normal like everyone else.

"Dan," I said to him, when we were in bed and the lecture was finally over, "why do you think she did it?"

Dan tried to caress my leg, then my arm, then my stomach, but I winced every time he touched me. He finally found a spot that was injury-free—my left breast—and did his best to express his love and concern on that small part of my body.

"I talked to the sheriff while you were getting stitched up. After Janet Macavity was given a pretty hefty dose of Demerol to take the edge off her pain, she started rambling like she was on truth serum. Although it won't be admissible in court, he found out quite a lot about her motives."

"Really! Tell me everything!" I suddenly felt better. At least around the left breast.

"Well, apparently she kept asking for her husband. The sheriff knew Janet wasn't married, but he finally asked his name."

"Did she give a name?"

Dan nodded. "First she said Michael Barnard."

"Never heard of him."

"Then she changed it to Burnett Pike."

"You're kidding! But he's married to Carrie Yates. Maybe she was confused by the drugs."

"That's what Sheriff Mercer thought at first. But she went on talking about their wedding in Florida and how happy they were, blah, blah, blah."

"Oh my God! He *is* from Florida....'

"The sheriff did some checking and found out Janet Macavity lived in Florida ten years ago. But she was married to a man named Michael Barnard at the time. His birth certificate says he was born in Florida, and his social security number lists his job as orderly at the Floridian Shores Hospital."

"But that's not the same man, right?"

"Let me finish." He tweaked my nipple. I yelped. He smiled. I tweaked his nipple back. He quit smiling. "Do you want to hear this or not?" he said, pouting.

"Go on!"

"Well, according to the marriage certificate, Michael Barnard was married to a woman named Janet Macavity, who also worked at the hospital as a nurse."

"But what does Michael Barnard have to do with this?"

"I'm getting there. Anyway, the next public record Sheriff Mercer found was a bit of a surprise."

"What? They got divorced?"

"No, they got arrested."

"What for? Drug dealing? Like Dakota?"

Dan looked at me. "I wouldn't try out for any game shows if I were you. You'd never make it on *Jeopardy!* You blurt too much."

"I don't blurt! I'm thinking aloud. And the drugs make sense, if you're going to somehow tie this into Dakota's murder."

"They were arrested for embezzlement."

"Stealing money from the hospital?"

"Nope. Making bogus hospital claims using deceased-patient information."

I tried to sit up. "Oh my God! Just like the scam that Holly suspected at Mother Lode Memorial!" It hurt. I lay back down.

"Bingo."

"Did they go to prison?"

Dan found another place to caress that didn't hurt. But it was distracting.

"Nope. The hospital didn't want a scandal. They asked for restitution instead of jail time. But Michael Barnard apparently committed suicide, leaving his wife, Janet, to take the full blame. She couldn't pay the amount back all by herself, so she was forced to go to prison after all. For seven years."

"Wow."

"When she was released, she moved to California and lied to get the job at Mother Lode Memorial, saying she'd been a housewife for the past seven years and had no public work record. Since she was only hired as clerk in the business office, the hospital never checked farther than that."

"So she worked her way up to director of the business office...."

"Yep."

"In charge of all that money..."

"You got it."

"But why was she asking for Burnett Pike? And this so-called husband who committed suicide?"

"Think about it."

"There was no suicide."

"Nope."

"And Michael Barnard, probably using the name of one of their deceased patients, slipped away with a new identity, and became..."

"Our own Burnett Pike."

It was a wonder I could work this all out, what with the location of Dan's hands by this time.

Chapter 27

THE NEXT MORNING I awoke with aching bones, muscles, tissues, flesh, and anything else that could feel pain. I also had a few dozen questions still unanswered. The aches and pains took priority, so I soaked in a hot bath while Dan made breakfast. The water offered both comfort and torture—an interesting combination. Some of my body parts relished the soothing warmth, other parts burned even at the gentle touch of the bath water. Kind of reminded me of the sex we'd had last night.

I picked up Casper first thing and treated her like a baby when I got her home. Steak breakfast. Fresh sleeping blanket. Annoying new chew toy that would always appear underfoot. She didn't seem terribly bothered by the missing toenail. I think it bothered me more than her.

After I got her spoiled and settled, I spent the rest of the day sorting through my heap of unanswered questions. The sheriff filled in some gaps and I deduced a few answers on my own. My biggest concern was Miah. Where had he been for the past two days while we'd been looking for him?

"Simonie's," Sheriff Mercer said, when I went to see him that afternoon.

"Dakota's ex-girlfriend's? What was he doing there?" I was stunned, to say the least. It felt as if he'd gone over to the other side.

"Seems he went over to talk with her and try to convince her that he didn't kill Dakota. At first she didn't want anything to do with him. Then after they started talking and comparing notes, Simonie finally admitted he must be telling the truth."

"What made her change her mind?"

"Miah was doing his own sleuthing while we were looking for him. He went over to Dakota's place and found a stash of drugs in his frog pond. It was buried under the water, in a waterproof container. No one thought to look there."

"Like father, like son," I said.

"What do you mean?" the sheriff asked.

"He'd make a great cop." The sheriff smiled. "Where is he now?"

"Home. He said he's going into the comic book shop this afternoon. And he knows he has a lot to catch up on at your newspaper. He feels real bad, but he figured he had to do something to clear his name. Guess he didn't trust us." Sheriff Mercer looked a little defeated.

"I don't think it was that, Sheriff. He's like me. We like to be in control, no matter how many competent people are trying to help us. I swear, if the pilot offered me a chance to fly the plane, I'd take the wheel away from him in an instant."

"I can imagine what Jeremiah must have felt," the sheriff said. "And by the way, it's called the stick, not the wheel."

"Well, tell him he's got a pile of work to do when he gets to the office. Find out anything else about Janet? Why she killed Dakota and tried to gas Holly and drown and strangle and blind me?"

"She won't say much. But Burnett had a few things to say, when I told him I knew the truth about his background and threatened him with an arrest."

"Did he explain why he was using a false name? And why he came out to California?"

"Like we figured, he faked a suicide to avoid dealing with the threat of restitution or prison. But he never forgot Janet. Or more to the point, he never forgot about the money she'd embezzled. Apparently she'd kept some. When she was released, she immediately left Florida, taking the money with her. Burnett started looking for her as soon as she got out."

"And he finally found her at the Mother Lode Hospital here in California."

"Yeah. Seems he traveled around for a while, working small scams by opening false businesses, taking in money through orders, then leaving town with the cash. When he finally found Janet, he figured they could pick up where they left off. By then he had a scheme for bilking the Mother Lode Hospital out of government money."

"And Janet agreed to this?"

"As a matter of fact, she didn't. Told him she wanted no part of his plan. But when he threatened to expose her, she knew it would cost her her job. She figured she had no choice. And the money she'd stolen was gone."

"So he wanted her to help him embezzle money by using false IDs to get federal and state funding for critical patients."

"Yeah, except there was one little problem."

"What?" I asked.

"Janet was *already* doing that."

"Evil minds think alike."

"Apparently she'd been caught at it, too. About nine months before."

"You're kidding! Who caught her? Dakota? Was he black-mailing her?"

"Nope. Carrie Yates's deceased husband, Monko. He found out when Janet tried to use the Medicare benefits of his GetWell patients, just before he died."

"Did he report her? Why didn't she get fired then?"

"Monko had a heart attack the next day."

"Holy shit!"

"My guess is, it was medically induced," the sheriff said. "No one ever checked for drugs. And that was just the beginning."

"So, Burnett arrived shortly after Monko died. But why did he marry the widow Yates?"

"That was Janet's idea. She convinced him to marry

Carrie, who was already in poor health, both mentally and physically, after Monko's death. She wanted Burnett to take over Carrie's GetWell business, thinking that would be an easier way to scam the money. Eventually they'd get rid of her and the business would be theirs. What Janet didn't tell Burnett, though, was that Carrie had been making threatening remarks to her."

"About Monko's death? Did she suspect something?"

"She said she knew Janet had killed him. She was a threat to Janet, and one way to keep her under control was to drug her. If Burnett married her, it would be an easy task to keep her medicated—and incoherent."

"That's why Carrie was so loopy all the time," I said. "She wasn't really that sick. She was drugged. And Dakota was her dealer."

"Yep. Her doctor had taken her off prescription drugs after her husband died. Dakota knew a potential customer when he saw one. He offered her more. And she took it."

"She couldn't get the kind of drugs she needed from her own center?" I asked.

"Not lithium. They had no patients there who required it. And that was her addiction."

"God! Dakota sure wasn't your average schoolyard dealer, was he? Seems like he supplied half the town with drugs."

"Apparently during one of Dakota's visits, Carrie was coherent enough to tell him of her suspicions about Janet Macavity. She still believed Janet killed her husband because of what Monko had discovered. He'd told Carrie about Janet's embezzlement before he died. She passed the information on to Dakota, to see if he would help her find evidence."

"Instead, Dakota took the information for his own use," I said.

Sheriff Mercer nodded. "He thought Janet was the only one involved in the scam and threatened to expose her—if she didn't start ordering more drugs for the hospital pharmacy. His demand was increasing and he needed more supplies."

"So she killed him."

"She killed Buford the Bullfrog first, to show him she meant business. Then she dumped some of his drug supply into the creek, to kill off the frog population, just to make the point. He was furious. He went to the creek that night to collect water samples to use as evidence against Janet."

"But Janet was watching him, wasn't she? She's certainly not stupid, to have come this far."

"She had drugged his water bottle sometime when he wasn't looking. Then she waited for the drugs to take effect so she could push him into the creek and hold him under until he drowned."

I shivered. The thought of my own watery near-death loomed in my mind.

"Wait a minute! All this time I thought Carrie was the one who tried to drown me. She was practically bathing in chili powder and I was sure she was the one who had pushed me in the water with her chili-covered hands. But it was Janet?"

"First of all, if you could smell the chili at the creek—and after—there was way too much to be accidental. Janet was a master at planning ahead. She went there deliberately to kill you—and to make it look like Carrie did it. They would have found the chili powder in your hair at the autopsy."

I shivered again. "You're right. It was way too obviously a plant. And I fell for it. She framed Miah, too. But why? Me, I was probably getting too close. But did she have something against Miah? Or maybe you?"

"She heard Dakota accuse him of killing his frog. It never occurred to Dakota that Janet did it as a threat. He found that out later, after the frogs started dying in the creek. He knew Miah wouldn't do *that*."

"So Janet used the opportunity to frame Miah. She put Miah's frog in Dakota's mouth to make it look like Miah took revenge on him." I thought for a moment. "What about Holly? Why did she try to kill her?"

"Holly was on to her, too. Janet was making too many mistakes. When Del Ores was at the hospital, Holly retrieved her chart—and found the chart of Eugene Stadelhofer on Janet's desk."

"Wow. What a story for the *Eureka!*"

Mayor Ellington entered the office carrying a box of chocolates. Was he here to make amends? It would take more than a box of chocolates to fix things with me. Like two boxes.

"Mayor, you found it." Sheriff Mercer held out his hand. The mayor passed him the box.

"Isn't that some kind of graft, Sheriff, taking chocolate from the mayor?"

The mayor cast me a cold glance. "You want to tell her, Sheriff?"

Sheriff Mercer opened the box. Inside were a dozen pairs of chocolate-covered frogs' legs.

"Yuck!" I said. "How disgusting."

"You sure you don't want to give her one, Sheriff?" the mayor said. He had an evil glint in his eye. Then again, when didn't he?

"You don't want one of these, C.W." He lifted one with a pair of tweezers he found in his desk. "They're laced with arsenic."

I gulped. "Where'd you find them?" I looked at the mayor. "Were they for you?"

Sheriff Mercer shook his head. "The mayor found them on the doorstep of the GetWell Center."

"They were meant for Carrie?"

"Nope, they were addressed to Burnett."

"What?"

The mayor spoke up. "They were a gift. From Janet Macavity."

Talk about tying up loose ends, I thought. No more chocolate-covered amphibians, insects, and other living things for me. Just the straight stuff from now on.

Critter's Creek was purified and restocked by the end of the week. It would soon make a healthy environment for future Jubilee contestants. The groundwater scare proved to be groundless. The medications dumped into the creek by Janet were diluted, washed away, and by now, harmless. There was no leakage from a neighboring institution polluting our drinking water. Thank God.

The annual Jumping Frog Contest of Calaveras County would continue, promised the mayor. As would the government funding for the disabled, albeit more carefully controlled in the future.

Burnett was arrested—this time he'd go to jail for sure—for his part in the scam with Janet Macavity, who was already locked up. He wasn't a murderer, but just short of that. He'd spend some time where the sun don't shine.

Holly got her son back almost immediately. After Burnett spewed everything, it was clear that Janet had tried to murder Holly and set it up to look like she overdosed. There was never any real threat to the mother–son relationship. Holly and Jonathan have been over a couple of times for dinner. Casper loves the little guy.

As for me, I learned a lot about blindness, something I had been blinded to with my own disability. Del Ores, like me, could do nearly anything—except drive a car, and I had a hunch she could even do that with a little guidance. My own fear of going blind lessened a little, after observing how normally Del Ores lived her life. In fact, I decided to learn Braille.

It's not an easy system to learn. But I practice it every day. Mainly on Dan's body.

Rebecca Warner

ABOUT THE AUTHOR

Penny Warner is the author of over twenty-five books, including five in the Connor Westphal mystery series. *Dead Body Language* was nominated for an Agatha award and won a Macavity award for Best First Mystery. With her husband, Tom, she writes and produces mystery fund-raisers for libraries and other organizations.

The holder of a master's degree in Special Education, Warner teaches child development and sign language at local colleges, and has taught infant and preschool deaf children. In addition, she teaches nonfiction and mystery writing at bookstores and various university and college campuses.

Penny Warner has two grown children and lives in northern California with her husband. She can visited at www.PennyWarner.com.

MORE MYSTERIES FROM PERSEVERANCE PRESS

Baby Mine, A Port Silva Mystery
by Janet LaPierre
The web of small-town relationships in the coastal California village is fraying, stressed by current economic and political forces. Police chief Vince Gutierrez and his schoolteacher wife, Meg Halloran, must help their town recover.

Royal Flush, **A Jake Samson & Rosie Vicente Mystery**
by Shelley Singer
Jake and Rosie infiltrate a dangerous far-right group, to save a good kid who's in over his head. The laid-back California private eyes will need a scorecard to tell the ringers in the gang from the real racist megalomaniacs.

Guns and Roses, **An Irish Eyes Travel Mystery**
by Taffy Cannon
Ex-cop Roxanne Prescott turns to a more genteel occupation, leading a History and Gardens of Virginia tour. But by the time the group reaches Colonial Williamsburg, odd misadventures and annoying pranks have escalated into murder.

The Kidnapping of Rosie Dawn, **A Joe Barley Mystery**
by Eric Wright
A Toronto academic sleuth goes on an odd odyssey, to rescue student/exotic dancer Rosie Dawn, and find out who wants her out of the way, and why. One part caper, one part satire, and one part love story compose this new series entry.

Forthcoming in 2001

The Tumbleweed Murders, **A Claire Sharples Botanical Mystery**
by Rebecca Rothenberg, completed by Taffy Cannon
Microbiologist Sharples explores the musical, geological, and agricultural history of California's Central Valley, as she links a mysterious disappearance a generation earlier to a newly discovered skeleton and a recent death.

Keepers, **A Port Silva Mystery**
by Janet LaPierre
Patience and Verity Mackellar, a mother-and-daughter private investigative team, unravel a baffling missing persons case and find a reclusive religious community hidden on northern California's Lost Coast.